A RIP VAN WINKLE OF THE KALAHARI

A RIP VAN WINKLE OF THE KALAHARI

SEVEN TALES OF SOUTH-WEST AFRICA

FREDERICK CORNELL

CruGuru

A RIP VAN WINKLE OF THE KALAHARI

ISBN: 978-1-920265-56-4

Originally published in 1915

This edition published by CruGuru in 2008

www.cruguru.com

Foreword

MOST of these stories were written on the veldt; at odd times, in out-of-the-way prospecting camps, in the wilds of the Kalahari Desert, or of that equally little-known borderland between Klein Namaqualand, and Gordonia, Cape Colony, and what was at that time known as German South- West Africa.

Four of them appeared a few years back in The State an illustrated magazine now unhappily defunct; the others, though written about the same time, have never been published.

And now, time and circumstances have combined to bring the scene in which they are laid most prominently before the public.

Through the dangerous and difficult barrier of the desert sandbelt that extends all along the coast, General Botha and his formidable columns forced their way to Windhuk; from the remote lower reaches of the Orange River other troops steadily and relentlessly pushed north; and even to the east the well-nigh unexplored dunes of the southern Kalahari proved no safeguard to the Germans, for Union forces invaded them even there: and all eyes in South Africa are to-day turned towards this new addition to the Union and the Empire.

Whilst imagination has naturally played the chief part in these tales, the descriptions given of certain parts of this little-known region are accurate, and by no means overdrawn; at the same time, though they treat principally of the dangerous and waterless desert, it must be borne in mind that although the sand dunes form one of Damaraland's most striking features, yet it is by no means altogether the barren, scorching dust-heap it is popularly believed to be.

For once the sand region bordering the coast is traversed, and the higher plateau begins, vegetation and water become more abundant, the climate is magnificent, and cattle, sheep and goats thrive; whilst in the north much of which remains practically unexplored there is much fruitful and well-watered country teeming with game, and akin to Rhodesia, awaiting the settler.

Mining and stock-raising are the two great possibilities in this new country, where water conditions are never likely to allow of extensive agriculture being carried out successfully.

But above all mining! For much of the country and especially the north is very highly mineralized. Copper abounds; tin and gold have been found and there can be but little doubt that the former will eventually be located in abundance and, above all, the diamond fields of the south-west coastal belt have since their discovery in 1908 added enormously both to the value of the country and to its attractiveness.

To refer again to these tales; the description of Rip Van Winkle's ride through the desert, the sand-storm, the huge salt "pans," and indeed most of the earlier incidents, have been but common-place experiences of my own in the wastes of the southern Kalahari, slightly altered for the purposes of the story. Even the "poison flowers" exist there and no Bushman will sleep among them, beautiful as they are. And lest the huge diamond in the head of the "Snake" in the same story be considered an impossibility, let it be borne in mind that the Cullinan (enormous as it was) was but the fragment of a monster that must have been every whit as big as the one I describe. The cataclysm is also a possibility; for although rain falls but seldom in the desert, there are occasional thunderstorms of extraordinary violence, and I have seen wide stretches of the Kalahari near the dry bed of the extinct Molopo River (long since choked, and part of the desert) converted into a broad deep lake, after a cloudburst lasting but an hour or so, which drowned hundreds of head of cattle.

The incident in "Dick Sydney," of the fracas in the bar where the Germans were toasting to "The Day," was not written after war was declared, but one night in Luderitzbucht full three years ago, after hearing that toast drunk publicly in the manner described, and after witnessing a very similar ending to it! And that particular story was refused by the then editor of The State, as being too anti-German! Well times have indeed changed!

And lest a prospective "Dick Sydney" should think that the picture of that individual picking up a thousand carats of diamonds in an hour or so is far-fetched, let me assure him that the first discoverers of the Pomona fields, south of Luderitzbucht, did literally fill their pockets with the precious stones in that space of time: and that other fields as rich may well await discovery will be denied by few who know the country.

"Ex Africa semper aliquid novo" never was saying truer! and Damaraland, under the British flag, and with scope given to individual enterprise, may well provide still another striking example of that old adage.

FREDERICK C. CORNELL.
Cape Town, 1915.

Table of Contents

1.   A RIP VAN WINKLE OF THE KALAHARI

INTRODUCTORY

The manner of my meeting with him was strange in the extreme, and a fitting prelude to the wild and fantastic story he told me.

I had been trading and elephant shooting in Portuguese territory in Southern Angola; and hearing from my boys that ivory was plentiful in German territory, farther south, I had crossed the Kunene River into Amboland; and here, sure enough, I found elephants and ivory galore. So good, indeed, was both sport and trade in this country of the Ovampos that by the time I reached Etosha Pau my "trade" goods had vanished, and my wagon was heavily laden with fine tusks. So far had I penetrated into German territory that I decided to make my way south-west towards Walfisch Bay instead of returning to Portuguese territory. But I knew I must rest my cattle well before attempting it, for it would mean an arduous trek; I had no guide, and there were no roads; for at the time I speak of, the Germans had done but little to open up the northern part of their territory; and indeed even to the present day much of it still remains unexplored.

It is a wild and beautiful country, for the greater part well-wooded, and teeming with game; though towards the east it becomes drier and sandier until there stretches before the traveler nothing but the endless dunes of the unknown Kalahari desert.

Untraversed, unexplored, and mysterious, this land of "The Great Thirst" had always held a great fascination for me; its outlying dunes began but a few miles east of my camp, and from an isolated granite kopje near their border I had often gazed across the apparently limitless sea of sand: stretching as far as the eye could reach to where the dancing shimmer of the mirage linked sand and sky on the far horizon.

It was along the edge of these dunes that I one day followed a wounded eland so far that dusk overtook me a long distance from my wagon. My water-bottle was full, there was abundance of dry wood for a fire, and I was just debating whether I would try and get back to the wagon, or camp where I was, when my horse solved the question for me by shying violently at something, and throwing me clean out of the saddle.

My head must have struck a stone, for I was stunned, and for a time I knew no more.

When I came to myself it was dark, but a bright fire was burning near me, a blanket covered me, and I was lying upon something soft. Evidently some one was caring for me, and I concluded that my boys had found me though I had given them strict instructions not to leave the wagon.

"Jantje! Kambala!" I called, but there was no answer, and I tried to rise. But my hurt had apparently been a severe one, for my head spun round, the fire danced before my eyes, and I again lost consciousness.

When next I awoke the fire was still burning, and a figure was seated beside it: a figure that the leaping flames rendered monstrous and distorted. The back was towards me, but at the slight rustle I made upon my bed of dry leaves in awakening, the figure turned in my direction, and I caught a momentary glimpse of the face. Firelight plays strange tricks sometimes, but the momentary flicker showed me a countenance so grotesque that I must have made an involuntary movement of surprise, for with a short laugh the unknown man rose and came towards me, saying as he did so, "Don't be scared even the devil isn't as black as he's painted!" And, whoever he was, the way in which he tended to my throbbing head, advising me not to talk, but to rest and sleep, soon soothed my shaken nerves, and I slept again till broad daylight.

I could hear the low murmur of voices, and sitting up, I saw that Jantje and Kambala had put in an appearance and were talking in an unknown tongue to my friend of the night before--a white man--but surely the strangest-looking being I had ever beheld.

First of all he was a hunchback, and his body was twisted and distorted to a remarkable degree yet in spite of his curved shoulders he was of more than average height, and of a breadth incredible. But his face! who can describe it? Seamed and scarred in deep gashes, as though by some hideous torture, the nose broken and flattened almost upon the cheek, there remained but little human about the awful countenance except the eyes. But these, as I found later, were of a beauty and expressiveness to make one forget their terrible setting. Large, pellucid, of a bright hazel, there was something magnetic in their straight and honest gaze; and I can well believe that before he met with his awful disfigurement their owner must have been a man of superb appearance.

As I moved, he came towards me, holding out his hand as he did so, and a fine, warm-hearted grip he gave me.

"Better, eh?" he said. "No don't get up; you've had an ugly smack, and must take care of yourself for a bit. And I'm afraid," he continued, as he sat down beside me, "that I was the cause of your accident for your horse shied at me, and you came near breaking your neck!"

"Shied at you?" I queried, in surprise for there was scarce cover for a cat just where I had been thrown "but where were you, then I never saw you?"

"No, but I saw you," he replied grimly, "and having been the cause of your downfall, I could do no less than look after you till your boys came."

Thus strangely began an acquaintance that lasted only all too short a time, but that was full of interest for me; for I found my new friend to be a remarkable man in more ways than in appearance. His knowledge of the region we were in was wonderful, the few natives we met treated him with every sign of respect and fear, and he seemed equally conversant with their language, as with that of my own boys, Jantje the Hottentot, and Kambala the Herero.

The habits of the game, the properties of each bush and shrub, each game-path and water-hole, he knew them all, and had something interesting to say about all of them; and the few days of our companionship were pleasant in the extreme.

I never knew his name, and had it not been that chance came to my aid, I should probably never have heard his strange history. But it so happened that a few days after our first meeting, a buffalo, with the finest horns I had ever seen, got up within twenty yards of us; and in my eagerness to secure his wonderful head, I shot badly, and only succeeded in wounding him slightly. His terrific charge was a thing to be remembered.

Straight at us he came, wild with rage, and my new friend's horse, gored and screaming, went down before him in a flash. The rider was thrown, and to my horror, before I could control my own frightened animal sufficiently to enable me to shoot, the bull was upon the fallen man, goring and trampling upon him in an awful manner. Leaping from my horse, I put bullet after bullet through the big bull's head, and at length he lurched forward, dead, upon the mangled body of his victim.

We had some difficulty in extricating the man, and never expected to find him alive, but though badly crushed and torn he still breathed, and naturally I did all I could to save his life.

That night he was delirious, and it was then that I had evidence of the almost superhuman strength with which he was endowed. Time after time he tore himself from the combined strength of my two sturdy boys, and always he raved of diamonds, and of a never-ending search for something, or some one, in the desert.

His hurts were sufficient to have killed half a dozen men, and I never expected him to live; but two days later he was able to tell the natives, in their own tongue, of certain herbs which they prepared under his direction, and in a week he was about again.

His cure was nothing short of miraculous in my eyes at least but he made light of his own share in the matter, and was all gratitude for the little I had been able to do to atone for the result of my bad shooting. And one night, by the camp fire, and with very little preamble, he told me the following strange story, which I have set down as nearly as possible in his own words.

I - THE BLUE DIAMOND

Diamonds first brought me to this country--a small glass phial full of them in the hands of an old sailor who had been shipwrecked on the South-west African coast, somewhere in the vicinity of Cape Cross, and who had spent many months wandering with the Bushmen who found him, before he eventually worked his way back safely to Walfisch Bay. Here one of the rare whalers, that occasionally called at that little-known spot, eventually picked him up, and he at length got back to Liverpool, with nothing but his tiny packet of little bright stones to show for all his months of hardship among the Bushmen.

The ignorant whalers had laughed at his assertion that the little crystals were of any value; as at that time diamonds were undreamed of in South Africa--for all this was long, long ago.

Chance threw me in the old man's way, and a small service I was able to render him led to his showing me the stones. He had been in Brazil and had seen rough diamonds there; and I too, who had also dug in the fields of Minhas Geraes, saw at once that he was right; they were diamonds.

I had money, but I wanted more; for there was a girl for whom I had sworn to make a fortune, and who in turn had sworn to wait for me, poor girl! She little knew how long that wait would be, or the kind of wreck that would return to her at last. And even as I poured the little glittering cascade of diamonds that old Anderson had found from one hand to the other, my mind was made up.

"Anderson," I said, "come out with me to Africa again, man; we can make ourselves rich men! Of course, there must be more where these came from?"

"More!" said the hard-bitten old seaman, who was as brown and withered as the Bushmen he had lived amongst so long; "More, is it? Why, sir, there's bushels of them in a valley as I knows of out there; so many that I couldn't believe myself that they was diamonds, so I only brought a few! But there they can stay for me. No more Bushmen for me, thank 'ee; they'd put a poisoned arrow through me if ever they saw me again. But if you want to go, well and good; I'll tell you where to find the diamonds!"

And the upshot was that I sailed for the Cape a week later, and a few months afterwards I landed at Walfisch Bay, from whence I intended trekking north in search of the Golconda old Anderson had described to me.

At that time, with the exception of a few traders, hunters, and missionaries near the coast, the country was uninhabited by white men; moreover, it was in a state of turmoil. From the north-east, a powerful Bantu race the Damaras, or Ovaherero as they term themselves had been gradually spreading over the land south and west, and had just come in contact with the Namaquas, a Hottentot race who had come from the south. The result had been a series of bloody native wars, in which neither race could for long claim decided advantage. Meanwhile the aboriginal Bushmen of the country had been almost exterminated, scattered tribes of them only remaining in the most inaccessible parts of the country. It was towards these wild people that my path lay, and the few settlers I met warned me that my trip was likely to be a dangerous one.

"And you have nothing to gain!" they pointed out, "these Bushmen have no cattle, no ivory, nothing! They are but vermin, and a poisoned arrow is all you are likely to get from them." But, secure in my knowledge of the riches awaiting me, I was not to be deterred; and there came a day when my wagon, loaded with a goodly stock of "trade" goods, trekked from the sands of Walfisch Bay towards the then unknown country lying to the north. Rain had fallen and I found the trek by no means as difficult as I had expected, for I had good native guides, and for a time all went well. But gradually the long sandy stretches were left behind, and the country became extremely difficult. On all sides rose vast table-topped mountains with almost perpendicular sides, and the wide valleys between them gradually narrowed till they became nothing but deep, narrow, precipitous gorges, impassable for a wagon. Deep we penetrated into this tangle of mountains, endeavoring in vain to find a way through in the direction I believed the valley to lie, and at length it became evident that to proceed farther with the wagon was out of the question. Here, therefore, in a well-wooded kloof, with an abundance of water, I made my central camp; and from it I proceeded to explore the country farther north. By this time the wild Bushmen, who had hitherto fled at our approach, had gained confidence, and came freely to the camp, and I had guides in plenty. For a time their extraordinary "click" language was utterly beyond my comprehension, but at length I learnt enough of it to make them understand what I wished to find.

But search as I would I could never find the spot--valley after valley they took me to, krantz after krantz, and kloof after kloof, I scrambled through and searched, but all in vain. Mineral wealth I found every-where, copper and tin in abundance, and in one deep valley rich nuggets of gold, but still the diamonds evaded me. Nor did I ever find them, though I am sure that Anderson's tale was true, and that somewhere in those mountains lie diamonds galore. It may be that they are now buried deep in the sand; for at times the wind blows with incredible force; and in the terrific sandstorms, huge dunes are lifted and swept across the country; and it may well be that the deep valley of his day is now filled to the level of its walls.

Sick and disheartened I determined at last to offer a big reward to any of the guides who should bring in a diamond to me; and calling them all together, I made them understand as much; at the same time show-ing one of the little diamonds that Anderson had given me. A trade musket, with powder and shot, was to be the reward; and as this was a prize beyond the dreams of these poor Bushmen there was a general exodus from the camp in search of the "bright stones." From their excited exclamations when I showed them the diamond, I gathered that they had all seen such stones, and I cheered myself with the hope that at last I should be rewarded for all my hardships. But, alas! They brought in "bright stones" truly bright stones in abundance but quartz crystals chiefly; bright, clear, and sparkling, but of course utterly valueless; and though I sent them out again and again, they brought nothing in of any value.

Amongst my boys, who had followed me from Walfisch Bay, was one Inyati, who was much attached to me, and who had become a sort of body-servant to me. He was a fine upstanding chap who held himself absolutely aloof from the Griquas and Hottentots that formed the bulk of my paid followers, and to whose oblique eyes, and pepper-corn wool, his expressive orbs and shock of crinkled hair formed an agreeable contrast. As for the Bushmen, Inyati treated them, and looked upon them, absolutely as dogs. He was a good game spoorer, and I had taught him to shoot; and so intelligent was he, that I had taken a great interest in him, and had learnt to talk to him in his own tongue a sonorous, expressive language entirely different to the peculiar "click" of the local natives.

I knew that his dearest wish was to possess a gun of his own, and fully expected that he too would wish to join in the search that might lead to his gaining one; but, though he had examined the stones I had shown far more intently than any of them, he made no effort to leave the camp. Day after day he attended to my simple wants, spending all his spare time in polishing my weapons, a work he absolutely loved, and crooning interminable songs in a low monotone.

One day, when the Bushmen had again trooped off on their fruitless search, I called Inyati; and told him to make certain preparations, as, should they again bring in nothing, I would strike camp and return to Walfisch Bay. And then I asked him, out of curiosity, why he had not tried to earn the gun.

"Master," said he, scraping away at the hollow shin-bone of a buck that served him as a pipe, as a broad hint that his tobacco was finished; "I know not the land of these dogs of Bushmen. If it were in my own land now! But that is far away!"

I laughed, for by his manner of saying it, he conveyed the impression that there he could pick up diamonds under every bush.

"Dogs they may be, Inyati," I answered him, "but they are dogs with keen eyes; and yet they cannot find the stones I seek, and that I know, too, are not far away!" He stood, nodding gravely at my words, and still fidgeting with his bone pipe; a splendid figure of a man, nude except for his leopard-skin loin-cloth, his skin clear and glossy, of a golden-brown for he was no darker than, but entirely different from, the yellow Hottentots.

"Master," said he; "what magic will my master make with the little bright stones, should he find them?"

"No magic, Inyati," said I, "but in my country, across the great water, these things are worth many muskets, cattle aye, and even wives!"

"That may be, my master," he replied, "but magic they are; and hide themselves when dogs such as these Bushmen search for them. Still, master, we will wait and see what they bring to-night; though well I know that they will come back with empty hands as empty as is this my pipe!"

I could not help laughing at the way in which he had brought the subject of his finished tobacco to my notice, and in a fit of unwonted generosity I not only gave him a span of tobacco, but also a cheap pipe from my "trade" goods.

Poor chap, it was the first he had ever had, for his shin-bone had served him hitherto, and his delight was unmistakable. An hour later I saw him still at his everlasting polishing, and with the new pipe in full blast; and now he was crooning not only its praises, but my own. Half his improvised song was unintelligible to me, but I understood enough to learn that when the "dogs of Bushmen" had failed, he, Inyati "The Snake" would lead me to a land where there were magic stones in abundance, and by means of which, I gathered, we should both obtain wives galore!

I laughed at the poor chap's foolish bombast, as I thought it; but I have often wondered since whether the gift of that cheap pipe did not, after all, alter the whole of my life.

For that evening, sure enough, the Bushmen again returned empty-handed, and acting on my former resolve, I called my own followers together, and told them to make ready to return to Walfisch Bay. Later, as I sat in my tent writing up my diary by the light of a feeble candle, and with the gloomiest of thoughts for company, I heard Inyati's voice outside. "Master," he said, in a low tone but little above a whisper, "the dogs are full of meat, and sleeping; and there is that which I would show thee."

Without feeling much interest in what he might have got I bade him enter, and he stood before me in the dim light of my tallow candle.

Fumbling in his leopard skin, he drew forth a little tortoiseshell, such as the Hottentot women use for holding the hare's foot, ochre, buchu leaves, and other mysteries of their toilet. I had often seen him with it, and had chaffed him about carrying it before, and he evidently anticipated something of the kind again.

"Nay, master," he said, before I could speak, "true, as thou sayest, it is a woman's box, and a woman gave it me. But the box is naught; this is what I would show my master."

He shook something from the little box into the palm of his hand, clenched it, and with a dramatic gesture thrust it close to the dim light, and threw his fingers wide.

There, glittering in the yellow palm, flashing and scintillating with every movement, and looking as though the light it gathered and reflected really burnt in its liquid depths, lay the most marvelous diamond I had ever beheld!

The size of a small walnut, flawless, blue-tinted, and of wondrous luster and beauty, its many facets were as brilliantly polished as though fresh from the hands of the cutter, though it was a "rough" stone, untouched except by nature.

I was too stunned to speak, or do anything but clutch it, and gloat over it, and mutter "Where? where?"

II - DEAD MEN IN THE DUNES

I don't know how long I gazed in fascination at the wonderful stone, but at length a low chuckle from Inyati brought me back to reality. He stood looking at me, with a whimsical smile on his face.

"Magic," said he, "magic, my master! Did I not say there was magic in these 'bright stones'? And who shall say it is not so? Has not my master for a whole moon been lifeless and sad, until he looked even as the old cow that died of lung-sick but yesterday? And has not the very sight of the magic stone again brought fire to his eye, till he is again even as the young bull that killed two of those Bushmen dogs also but yesterday? Who shall say it is not magic?"

"Inyati," I stammered, coming back to my senses, and ignoring his extremely doubtful compliments, "speak, man; where did you get this?"

"In my own land, master; a far land, many moons' trek from here, and where there are many. But few dare touch them except indeed the devil- men and they are not men at all, but devils! Though I feared them little even then . . . and now, now that I have a gun (for surely my master will give me the little gun that speaks many times for this magic stone?) I fear them not at all! And we will go back and get many more if my master so wishes and I will see again the woman who gave me the stone as a talisman long years ago!"

Give him "the little gun that speaks many times" the Winchester for a diamond worth a king's ransom?

"Inyati," I said, though I was sorely tempted, "the gun is thine; not indeed for the stone, for that I will not take from thee, and it is worth more than all the guns and cattle I possess. But for the gun, guide thou me to this land of thine, that I may find these stones thou callest magic."

"That will I do readily, master," he answered, "and, in truth, I am well content to keep the stone, for the sake of the woman who gave it me. And there are many more! And did I not say truthfully that the stones were magic? See now, my master, the very sight of one has made my master give me the desire of my heart the little gun that speaks many times."

I gave him the Winchester there and then, and never did I see a human being so delighted.

Late into the night we sat and talked, and planned, whilst the Bushmen sat round their camp fire, and clucked and chattered in their queer-sounding speech, gorging themselves to repletion on the offal of an eland I had shot the previous day.

I learnt that Inyati's country lay far to the north-east, across the dreaded waterless stretches of the unknown Kalahari. He had fled from it years ago, his life forfeit to the priests or "devil-men" as he called them for some cause that he did not explain, or that my limited knowledge of his language did not permit of my understanding. The stones were plentiful, that he assured me of again and again, but they were sacred, or tabooed, and no one was allowed to handle them but the priests of whom he spoke.

He had always wanted to return, but had always Feared, but now with his "little gun" I believe Inyati would cheerfully have faced a thousand priests, or for the matter of that a thousand warriors. Danger there would be, but what was that to him and his master?

He could find his way back, though the journey would be long and difficult; and now was the only season in which it could be undertaken; the season when the wild melon made it possible to traverse the waterless wastes of the "Great Thirst Land."

I did not hesitate a moment, in fact no wink of sleep had I that night, but lay tossing and turning, longing for daylight to come that I might inspan and commence my long trek.

It came at last, my preparations for striking camp were soon made, and sending off my crowd of Bushmen camp-followers with a small present of tobacco, I turned my back to the sea and began my long journey to the north-east.

Out of the long defiles and valleys we threaded our way into the open country, past the huge flat-topped mountains of Ombokoro, the fastness of the Berg Damaras, thence following the dry river-bed of the Om-Mafako north-east to the confines of the Omaheke desert that great north-western outlier of the true Kalahari not far, indeed, from this very spot! So far the trek had been slow and tedious, but without untoward incident. We were well armed, and those natives who did not avoid us were only too eager to bring in food, or show us water in return for our trade goods.

But, as the broken, bushy country gave way to the sand, water became scarcer and scarcer, until it could only be obtained in small quantities by digging deep in the bone-dry bed of the parched-up river.

At length it became evident that we could take the wagon and oxen no farther; and so, at some Bushmen water-pits, at the every edge of the desert, where "toa" grass and other fodder was still plentiful, I decided to leave both vehicle and beasts in charge of my Hottentot and Griqua followers, and attempt the desert journey on horseback, and accompanied only by Inyati. Indeed there was no other course; for the few "pans" that might contain water on the route we should have to follow, were far between, and, as the season was late, even they might well be dry. "T'samma," therefore, the wild melon that serves for food and water for both man and beast in these desert stretches, would be our only resource; but even in this respect the lateness of the season was a source of anxiety, for, as you doubtless know, when once it is over-ripe the t'samma is useless.

Two riding and two pack horses were all therefore that we dare take; on the latter we loaded food, ammunition, spare arms and trade goods; and with our skin water-bags filled, one evening when the moon was nearly at its full, we bade goodbye to our little band, and struck due east across the desert.

Our plan was to hold in that direction as long as t'samma was abundant; and should it fail, to attempt to reach one of the "pans" Inyati had discovered in his flight across the desert years before, and which the strange instinct of locality common to all natives of these wastes would probably enable him to find again.

All night long we rode slowly and steadily through the dunes which were here favorable to our course; for their long parallel lines ran like the waves of the sea, almost due east and west, as far as the eye could reach, and we were able to ride in the "aars" or narrow valleys between them and make good progress.

So far vegetation of a sort was still abundant, tufted "toa" grass, sorrel, and other succulent plants offered juicy fodder for the horses, and I began to think that this much-dreaded desert was a desert but in name, and that our task was to be a light one. With dawn we off- saddled. From the summit of a high dune I looked round in all directions, and as far as the eye could reach could see nothing but the endless monotony of wave after wave of dunes, treeless, and apparently almost devoid of vegetation, for the little there was, was confined to the deep hollows between. A short distance away a fair-sized bush offered a modicum of shade, and here we rested for the day for we had planned to travel only in the cool of the night as long as the moon served. And here Inyati showed me how to make water from the young green t'samma, taking those the size of an orange only, and roasting them in the ashes, and thus turning their pulp into a clear liquid like water. Seldom though did we trouble to do this, eating the insipid cucumber-like fruit as we found it, but though refreshing and capable of supporting life, the longing for water is always present in the desert.

And thus, trekking by night, and resting by day as much as the terrific heat would allow, we worked our tedious way into the heart of the desert; and now the magnitude of the task before me was becoming more fully apparent every day. For, toil as our willing beasts would, it was obvious that each long night's exhausting trek barely carried us ten miles forward as the crow flies. The dunes were each day becoming higher, till they were veritable mountains of sand, the patches of t'samma became less and less frequent, and it was evident that at any time they might fail altogether. All this time we saw no sign of human life, not even a solitary spoor upon the tell-tale sand. Animal life, however, there was in abundance, and we had no need to leave our path to shoot as much game as we required.

At times, on cresting the brow of a dune, we would come close upon a herd of gemsbok in the long "aar" beneath us; magnificent animals, whose long, straight, saber-like horns are feared even by the lion. Fearless of man, the whole troop would stand as one, gazing straight at us, immovable as statues, until we were within a few yards of them; then their leader, usually a magnificent bull, with horns of well on to four feet, would give a toss of his head and a stamp of his foot, and away the whole troop would fly; wheeling, trotting, halting and turning to gaze at us again, in such perfect unison, that they reminded one irresistibly of a well-drilled troop of cavalry.

Or a flock of ostriches would career across our path, their huge strides covering the ground at an incredible pace; queer-looking hartebeest were also plentiful, and duiker, steenbok, and smaller fry abounded everywhere.

Of lions we saw but little, though their spoors were abundant, and occasionally we heard them at night; the spoors of leopards were everywhere but these wily animals are seldom seen unless hunted for and often a pack of the dreaded wild hunting-dogs would stream across our path in pursuit of its quarry.

For strangely enough all of these animals appear to be absolutely independent of water, and some of them notably the gemsbok, apparently never drink.

There came a day when we entered an entirely different region, though still the sand stretched in all directions. But now the dunes were no longer either uniform in height or parallel as they had been, but tossed and tumbled in all directions in the utmost confusion; and here also t'samma, and in fact all vegetation, ceased. We reached this region of awful desolation a little after sunrise one morning, coming upon it abruptly from the edge of a dune whose hollow held the usual vegetation in plenty.

With my field-glasses I scanned the bare and barren waste before us in all directions, but no sign of life or vegetation broke the monotony of its awful desolation. I looked at Inyati, peering from under his palm in the same direction, and he answered my unspoken question.

"Yes, master, we must cross it. It runs for many days' journey north and south, and we cannot go round. I crossed it when I came, but farther south; and I found a little t'samma then. And yet I nearly died!"

That day the heat was very great, and here there were no bushes to give us a particle of shade. A few stunted "gar-boomen" there were, and the horses ate eagerly of the long bunches of bean-like fruit hanging from them; but their thin, withered foliage was no protection against the terrific power of the sun. Then Inyati showed me a Bushman trick; for, burrowing in the side of the dune, he soon made a considerable hollow, and breaking down the brittle "gar" bushes he roofed it over, throwing a whole pile of other bushes on top till it was light-proof enough to at least break some of the sun's glare.

And into this we crawled, and stewed till evening brought us some little respite.

Meanwhile we had discussed our chances of getting across.

"Three days, at least, my master, it will take the horses; and if we find no t'samma they will die. It is drier than when I crossed. But if we go not east, but turn somewhat to the south, there is a pan. It is two days only but who knows if there is water there? Still, mayhap, that is the better path." That night we had to wait late before trekking, as the moon was waning, and in the hideous jumble of dunes before us, we feared to trust solely to the stars. We were glad to rest too, and let our horses rest and take their fill of the last t'samma they were likely to get.

I lay smoking in the dark, waiting for the moon to rise, and listening to the "crunch, crunch" of the horses still steadily feeding, when a low call from Inyati made me spring to my feet, He had climbed to the top of the highest dune, and at his second call I ploughed my way up through the loose sand till I stood beside him. He was pointing away to the south-east.

"A fire, master," he said; "there are men there; that must be our way, for there must there be t'samma, or water!"

Sure enough a tiny fire was flickering far away, and apparently on the far horizon, though it is almost impossible to judge of the distance of a fire by night.

At any rate, it certainly seemed better for us to try to make our way to it, and without waiting longer for the moon we saddled up and started our floundering way across the labyrinth of dunes in its direction.

All night long we followed the faint gleam, which faded and vanished as morning found us, well-nigh exhausted, in the midst of the wilderness of bare sand.

But, though I could see nothing, Inyati's keen eyes made out a thin wreath of smoke from a prominent dune still some distance away; and in spite of our fatigue we struggled on, till, with the sun glaring down full upon us, we stood on the flank of the huge slope of sand. Near its crest, a few dry and blackened stumps and withered bushes showed where a little vegetation had once existed, and from near them rose the smoke. There was, however, no sign of life; and not a sound broke the awful silence of the desert, as we breasted the rise. Then a vulture flapped lazily up in front of us, and another and another and a tiger- wolf (hyena) lurched its gorged and ungainly carcass down the farther slope.

The fire was alive, but those that had built and lit it were dead . . . of thirst.

They lay there, all that the vultures had left, a fearsome sight; and their swollen and protruding tongues told the tale as plainly as though they had spoken. Yellow bodies, emaciated, but the bodies of what had once been a splendidly proportioned man and woman no Bushmen these!

"They are of my folk," said Inyati gravely, as he stooped to examine them, "mayhap they too have fled from the priests? . . And they have crossed the desert the way we would go and are dead of thirst!"

III - THE SAND-STORM

We scraped a hasty grave in the sand for the poor remains, and stood gazing silently across the dunes in the direction that the fresh spoors showed the two poor creatures had come from; stood there regardless of our fatigue, and of the blazing heat, of everything in fact but the grim tragedy before us, and the terrible significance it bore for us, who would follow the same path.

"We must rest, and eat," at length said Inyati, "so too must the horses, or they may die before there is need."

We stripped the loads from the poor brutes, and divided the bags of t'samma we had piled upon them, and soon they were munching away contentedly, whilst we rigged up some sort of shelter and lay and panted till the evening.

Then, and then only, did we discuss what we were next to do. "Master," at length said Inyati, "think, and think well. To go back is still easy, to go forward may well be that we die even as these two have died!"

"The desert is drier than when I struggled through it, more dead than alive, by the path these people came by and that way it would be madness to try! South, we might find another path, but it will be a longer one and . . . my master can still return. And the stone that my master can take and I will go on and bring him more, if he will but return to the camp and there await me. . . . And if I come not in two moons, I shall be dead. . . ."

He held out the blue diamond as he spoke; but the offer, genuine as it undoubtedly was, acted as a taunt to me, and I bade him sternly put back the stone, and talk not to me of returning.

"Thou sayest that the desert is but beginning," I told him. "Am I then a weakling, to run back like a whipped hound, at the sight of a dead man? Nay, I will return with the stones I seek, or not at all!"

Inyati nodded his head sagely as he sucked at his cherished pipe.

"Aye! Aye!" he said softly. "Said I not that the stones were magic? Sad, even as a sick cow, was my master, till I showed him the stone, and now he is even again as a young bull!"

If he had meant to stir me from the apathy that the desert had brought upon me, he certainly succeeded, for his complimentary comparison of me to a sick cow again set me laughing! It was the first time I had laughed for days, and it did me good.

"Yes, we must go south," said Inyati, "but not far. Only half a march, and then we will turn again east. Thus shall we find the pans."

That night we did not wait for the moon, but saddled our still jaded nags before it was well dark, and walking most of the way to rest them, we set our faces towards the Southern Cross. Half way through the night we halted, and resting for a while, again pushed on, but this time due east. Dawn found us eagerly looking round for a change in the landscape if a featureless chaos of tumbled sand is worthy of such a name? but I, at any rate, could see nothing.

Not so Inyati; his eyes were better than my field-glasses.

"Look, master!" he said, as the sun rose, "there, and there, and there! little low clouds, just rising from those three places and they won't last long! They are pans, master, and it is mist that rises from them. There is moisture there may be water there."

"And food for the horses?" I asked him; for our poor brutes were in an awful state, and we had nothing to give them.

"That may well be," he said, "not on the pans, but near them. And, master, we must struggle on, and find out; for they cannot fast another day, and trek another night, without either food or drink."

The rising sun rapidly dispersed the little clouds that Inyati had pointed out, but we kept on in their direction, though the sand was now burning hot and the poor animals were suffering frightfully.

Now a few scattered bushes and tufts of bone-dry "toa" grass began to show in the hollows between the dunes, and at length, on breasting an unusually high one a veritable mountain of sand, three or four hundred feet in height a new and marvelous scene stretched before me.

Abruptly from the foot of the steep dune-slope stretched a vast, glittering expanse of the purest white; to all appearance a snow- covered lake, spotless and dazzling in the brilliant sunshine. It was almost a perfect circle in shape and several miles in diameter, and on all sides it was hemmed in by gigantic dunes.

"Salt, master!" said Inyati. "I have seen such places before, but, wow! this is a big one! And this is not the pan I seek. No good to us, master; but is it not strange? Yonder in my land this salt is a precious thing; for a basketful, one can obtain a fat cow, for a sackful, two or more young wives! Here is salt enough to buy many wives, master; but none to gather it or for that matter, no wives to buy! . . . But water, master, is what we seek, and not salt water or t'samma. . . . We must cross, master; there on the other side I see thick bush in the dunes, there may be t'samma there, and the way across is easy. Come!"

He led the way down the steep slope, dragging his jaded animals after him. At the edge, where sand ended and salt began, lay many bones, bleached and white almost as the salt itself, and amongst them were the bones of men. Snorting and afraid, the animals stepped gingerly on the smooth, snow-like surface, which yielded but an inch or two to their tread, and was pleasantly cool to their hooves, parched and cracking from their long trek in the burning sand. Beneath the white surface was a moist black mud, and the liquid brine oozed quickly into the horses' footprints. Used as we were to the glare of the sun on the burning sand, here it was literally blinding, and long before we reached the farther side we were groping and stumbling like blind men. It was much wider, too, than it had first appeared, and we were utterly exhausted when at long length we reached the dunes again, and to our joy found bush, and a few t'samma, most of them old and hard, but still enough green ones to provide a scanty meal for the suffering animals. A respite it was, but a respite only, and well we knew that we must push on or return at once. Our water bags still held enough to keep us alive a day or two, but we must find water or t'samma for the horses soon, or it was evident they could not last. We threw ourselves down on the burning sand, with a blanket stretched over a tiny bush affording scant shade for our heads, and in spite of the roasting heat I slept the sleep of utter exhaustion.

I awoke to find Inyati afoot, and intent on adjusting the blanket to shade my face from the setting sun. I got up, aching and throbbing in every part of my body, and parched with a thirst that the lukewarm and already vile-tasting water from our skin bags did little to alleviate.

"Master," said Inyati, looking at me with concern, "take thou of the bitter powder (quinine); and sleep again. Before morning I will come back. For I must seek the pan I know of, where water may be found. This cursed salt pan I did not see when I crossed before: the pan I know is one of the others we saw the clouds rise from; which I know not? So I seek the nearest, and if water is there, by moonrise I will be here again. If not, and I must seek the farther one, then when the sun stands a span high I will be back. Nay, better that I should go alone; rest, master, and let the horses rest too, for if I find not the water, our path will be a hard one!"

He shouldered his Winchester, and strode off, all my arguments failing to persuade him to take a drop of our little remaining store of water. I watched him striding away through the dunes till he was lost to sight, then I turned to and made a fire and some food; for I felt weak and ill and my head was burning. Then I looked to the horses, hobbling them short in case they should stray though, poor brutes, they were too worn out to be likely to do anything of the kind. Then I gathered all the dry stumps and bush I could find, and made a fire, for lion and leopard spoor were very plentiful: moreover, a fire would help Inyati to find his way back. Later, as night fell, I lay down and tried to sleep; but exhausted as I was I could not rest. My thoughts were with Inyati. Would he find the pan and water? And if not, what would happen? The horses would scarce be able to struggle back to the nearest t'samma we had left, and in any case, to go back, beaten! No, if Inyati gave any hope at all, I would push on as long as life lasted.

So I lay and mused by the flickering fire, listening for the occasional yelp of a jackal, or the horrible laughter of a hyena.

Sleep I could not; the horses too were restless, snorting and fidgeting as they bunched close together, only a yard or two from where I lay.

I wondered if lions were prowling near, but could hear or see nothing. The air was hot and stifling, and there was none of the pleasant coolness usual to even these summer nights in the desert, and on climbing to the crest of the dune to look vainly towards where Inyati must be wandering, I saw that the sky in that direction was heavy with clouds; and even as I looked, flash after flash of lightning rent their heavy pall.

"Thank God!" was my first thought, "there will be rain there, and if the pans lie there, we shall find water."

I stood and watched for some time, and saw that the storm was traveling towards me, but it was still far distant, and I returned to the fire and again tried to sleep, for the moon would not rise for several hours, and Inyati had said he could not be back before then.

And this time I slept, a heavy sleep full of distorted dreams.

At length I awoke with a start, just as a gust of wind caught the fire and scattered the embers in all directions. Another and another followed, each more violent than the preceding one, then came a terrific blast that whirled the blanket I had been lying on away into the night: the last firebrand was snatched up as though by an unseen hand, and borne high over the dune, and before I had time to realize what was happening I was fighting for my life in the howling darkness of a terrific sandstorm. The wind was demoniacal; it apparently blew from all quarters at once, in short, sharp, incessant gusts, lifting and whirling away everything that came in its path, shifting the loose sand in such masses, and hurling it with such force that to stand still would have meant being buried. Luckily the scanty vegetation where we had rested had somewhat bound the sand, but in a few minutes of the awful struggle I realized that unless I could reach some firmer spot I must be overwhelmed. A momentary lull showed me the horses half buried, and apparently too stupefied to do more than stand passively awaiting their fate.

The salt pan! That was my only chance: there, at least, the very ground would not dissolve beneath my feet, as it was doing here! And I must make for it at once, for the whirling cataclysm of sand was again closing upon me. Seizing the horses I cut their hobbles, and throwing one of the packs across the nearest I coaxed and dragged him from the sand. I had my rifle, and I had no time for anything else, but made off in the direction of the pan, barely fifty yards away; but so terrible was now the force of the wind that I was hard put to it to reach it, and thankful indeed was I when a brief lull showed me the wide expanse of white spreading dimly before me in the murk.

Even here the ever-recurring whirlwinds bore huge volumes of sand eddying across the pan, and at times I feared I should be choked and overwhelmed, but as I gradually neared the centre the air grew clearer, and I knew that for the time, at least, I was safe.

The horses had struggled out after their leader, and stood trembling near me; luckily I had left them saddled and bridled in anticipation of an early start, but the other pack was lying there in the dunes. And thus I awaited the abatement of the storm, a prey to the most awful suspense.

Inyati! There in the distant dunes if the storm had caught him in their midst he must be dead, overwhelmed and buried in the chaos of sand! Or had he been able to gain one of the pans first; and would the abatement of the storm see him return to me?

Hour after hour I waited, and still it raged; the time for moonrise was long since past, though no gleam of its waning light could break through the whirling pall around me. Moonrise! That had been the time Inyati had hoped to return by, should he find water in the first pan; but where was he now, battling for his life among the dunes, or dead beneath them?

At length day dawned; and with the light the storm ceased as suddenly as it had begun, though still huge clouds of dust hung all around, through which the rising sun gleamed red and ray-less, as through a thick fog.

Soon not a breath of wind remained, and the dust rapidly settling, disclosed the tossed and distorted wilderness through which the storm had raged.

At no great distance from me, and, as I judged, in the direction of the spot at which the storm had overtaken me, a gigantic dune lay piled high above the others. This was some of the devilish work of the past night, for it had not been there yesterday!

There appeared no likelihood of a return of the storm; and, full of anxiety and distress, I made my way to this newly-formed dune, which apparently covered the exact spot of our camp of overnight; but now no vestige of bush remained in sight anywhere: it was all buried fathoms deep in sand. And gone too were many of our belongings, for with the exception of the one pack-saddle, to which one of the water-skins was providentially made fast, I had had no time to pick up anything; and now the half of our precious water, and much of our stores and ammunition, were covered by the thousands of tons of the gigantic dune. Search as I could, in all directions, I could find no trace of them, they had gone irretrievably; and gaze as I could from the highest point of the new dune I could see no sign of life, and the sad conviction was forced upon me that Inyati had perished, and that I was alone.

IV - THE PANS AND THE POISON FLOWERS

By this time the sun was high in the heavens, and I realized that if I would make a bid for life I must do it soon. Buffeted and almost choked with the battle of the past night, I was parched with thirst, and had perforce to encroach upon the scanty store left to me a bare quart at the outside; barely sufficient to keep life in me another day in the terrible heat. The horses, too, were suffering and would scarcely last that time, and I was now faced with the terrible problem as to whether I should attempt to return or to penetrate farther into the desert. To return would be difficult, for the storm had passed that way and all our spoors would be obliterated; moreover, we had gone out of our path so far when following the fire that I was by no means certain as to the absolute direction. Moreover, a glance that way showed me heavy, dun- colored clouds on the far horizon: there the storm was raging still, and I shuddered to think of what my fate might be in the loose bare dunes we had passed through with such difficulty. Besides, though Inyati's awful fate appeared but too certain, I felt impelled to follow the direction he had gone for there might, after all, be a faint hope that he had lived through the storm. But this alternative was a terrible one, for even if water had existed in the pans for which he was searching, it was all too probable that the storm would have filled up every pit with sand, and to penetrate so far would make return impossible. However, I could not remain where I was and die without a struggle; so, dividing the load as well as possible among the almost exhausted animals, I again entered the maze of dunes and struck due east, full of forebodings as to my own possible fate, and of sorrow for that of poor Inyati. For hours I stumbled through the bewildering mass of broken and barren dunes, finding no trace of vegetation, and full of apprehension lest the wind should rise before I reached the pan; in which case I was doomed. At long length, and when the afternoon was well advanced, a flat dark space showed between two dunes some distance ahead, and an hour later I stood upon the pan. No salt pan this time, but a flat, circular floor of dry mud, hard and entirely free from the surrounding sand. Here and there a few stunted bushes grew, and in the centre of the circle which was about a mile across stood a huge herd of gemsbok. They made off at a canter as I rode wearily across to the depression in the centre where I hoped to find water. But the shallow, hoof-trampled hollow was bone-dry; there was no sign of Inyati either, and my heart sank as I realized that my struggle had been in vain. Anyway, here I must rest and eat, and drink a little of my tiny stock of water, and on the morrow make my last struggle on foot, for it was evident that the horses could go no further, and were dying of thirst. I threw off their light loads, and they stood with drooping heads and ears, the picture of dejection. A mouthful of water was all I dare drink, and there remained less than a pint in the water-skin. Almost stupefied, exhausted, and despondent, I lay down beside a tiny bush, at whose dry twigs the famished horses were now trying to nibble, and sank into a state of half sleep, half stupor.

The sound of a shot aroused me from my lethargy had I been dreaming? No there it was again; and now across the pan came streaming back the herd of gemsbok, and after them ran and stumbled a nude black figure, that now and again paused to single out an animal and shoot.

"Inyati! Inyati! Thank God!" I cried out, for it could be no other; and as fast as my aching limbs allowed I hastened towards him. Now he was down beside one of the fallen animals, and his knife was at work; and now I realized why he had picked his victims, and had shot so many. It was not food he wanted, but drink, and he had shot only the cows, whose udders were full of rich sweet milk. It was time, too, that he drank, for he could not speak, and his cracked and swollen lips and blood-shot eyes told a tale of awful suffering.

Soon, however, he was able to talk. "The storm, master," he said; "near was I to being buried alive and I thought thee dead! Yet, could I not return before, for I have found no water. The other pan is dry also, but now I have seen from far off a spot where water is, and so I hastened back to find my master. It is far, but we shall win through." Caught by the storm between the two pans he had been hours staggering through the raging chaos, and had reached the pan only after the sun had risen and the storm had ceased to find it without a vestige of water.

Casting about in the dunes, he had searched for t'samma without avail, and filled with anxiety for me had been torn between a desire to return at once, and the absolute necessity of finding water. Hurrying from one prominent dune to another he had scanned the desert in all directions, and had even found one or two more pans, but again waterless. One, however, showed that it had held water recently for it was still moist, and there he had found a flock of the tiny Namaqua partridge, so plentiful in certain parts of the desert. These little birds are swift of flight, and fly long distances in search of water; and Inyati, as they rose in a cloud from their old drinking place, had marked the direction of their flight. North-east they went, and his keen eyes had followed them till they were no longer visible, and as he watched he saw many other flocks, and all flying in the same direction. "There is the water," thought Inyati, and he had toiled on in their wake, but the way was far, and it was hours before, from a high dune, he had seen a large pan in the distance, to which all the birds were converging. "A big pan, master," he said, "with thick bush and big trees an oasis or perhaps who knows? a river bed." And frantic with thirst as he was, he had not gone on, but turned back hoping to find me alive.

My heart leapt with joy at the news, for with the knowledge that water awaited us we could struggle on but the horses? Inyati shook his head as he examined them. "That one will die before morning," said he, "but maybe we can save the others, though they cannot carry us. We must eat, drink, and sleep, for the way is long and we are weak. And now, master, if all the tobacco is not there under the big dune with the other packs, I will smoke, for I have missed my tobacco sadly."

How he enjoyed himself, this lighthearted philosopher of the desert! Long steaks of tender gemsbok he cut and grilled on the wood ashes of the tiny fire, treating in a like manner the juicy udders after he had squeezed out most of the milk. The water he would not touch, but his appetite seemed unappeasable; steak after steak disappeared and still he carved and cooked, smoking between whiles, and singing some never-ending song of all the fine wives he would buy, and what he would do to certain priests, if he got his "little gun" safe to his own country. His cheery presence, and the reliance I placed in him cheered me enormous-ly, and I realized that I, too, was hungry. And so we ate, and smoked, and slept, till nearly midnight; and then, keeping the Southern Cross low down on the horizon on our right, we once more entered the dunes.

The horse that Inyati had referred to was obviously dying, and a mer-ciful bullet put an end to the poor brute's sufferings. The others trudged wearily after us, making but slow progress, but doing better than I had conceived possible of animals that had not eaten or drank for thirty-six hours. But morning found them dead beat; they stood stock still as the sun rose, and neither coaxing nor flogging could get the poor brutes a step farther. According to Inyati's reckoning we were still four hours from the water, and it was obvious that once we left them we could never hope to save them, for we could never bring back enough water to keep them alive.

"There is but one thing," said Inyati, as he slipped their loads off. "Water we cannot bring them, nor would it be in time, for once the sun is hot they will die. But stay here, and I will search for a certain thing. Nay, master," he continued, for I had made a gesture of dissent; "this time I go not far. But here I see rain has fallen of late, and though there is no t'samma, there may be another thing that will save the horses."

"Then I will seek it with you, Inyati," I said, for I was determined not to lose sight of him again.

"Better rest, master," he urged, "there will be no more sandstorms. And there is still far to go."

But go I would, and so we left the poor horses standing in a forlorn little group, gazing with sad lack-luster eyes at the masters who had brought them to such a plight. Inyati took with him a canvas bag that had been used as a saddlecloth, and I wondered what he hoped to find to fill it, for there was no vestige of vegetation to be seen, except some tiny seeds just sprouting here and there in the hollows between the dunes.

I could see no other evidence of the rain that Inyati spoke of, but soon, in a deeper depression than usual, we found signs that water had recently accumulated there, though the spot was now as dry as the surrounding dunes. But here Inyati, who had been keenly examining the ground, uttered a grunt of satisfaction, and pointed to a spot close to his feet. There was no trace of a plant, but a slight swelling, as it were, of the soil, which showed, too, some small cracks as though something was trying to burst its way to the surface.

"Cameel-brod," said he, and kneeling down he commenced scooping away the sand with his hands, and from a few inches below the surface he soon drew a whitish tuber the size of a large turnip. It was full of thin watery juice, acrid and sharp to the taste, but as I afterwards found, extremely acceptable to the horses.

Soon we had the bag nearly full, and cutting them up on our water-proof ground-sheet, we quickly had a quantity of watery pulp, at which the animals nuzzled greedily, and which revived them to a remarkable extent almost at once; so much so indeed, that we had very little difficulty in hurrying them forward again. The last drop of water had long since gone, and I was now consumed with thirst, and sick with misgiving as to what might be found at the pan Inyati had seen. Now we could see it, and, as yesterday, the flocks of partridges were all flying in that direction. How I envied them their wings, and how I grudged them the precious water they would be drinking! At length, footsore, weary, with eyes scorched by the blinding glare of the sun on the bare sand, and with lips cracked and tongues swollen with thirst, we staggered out of the dunes into a wide pan covered with bush and sprinkled with big trees huge cameel-doorn of thick verdant foliage, which gave the whole expanse a park-like appearance. They were full of gay-plumaged birds, butterflies were flitting everywhere, here and there were fine stretches of thick grass, in fact, after all we had suffered in the furnace of shade-less sand behind us, the place was a veritable paradise. And at length, where the trees were thickest, we espied tall green reeds growing thickly, and a few minutes later our fears were at an end, for here was water in plenty.

It was thick and muddy, and fouled by wild animals, whose spoors showed thick all around it; but to us it was absolute nectar, and it needed all Inyati's persuasion to prevent me from drinking to excess and probably dying on the spot.

We had to control the horses too, and let them drink but little at a time, or they too would probably have drank till they dropped dead in their tracks.

In this pleasant oasis we stayed for three days, resting, recuperating, and living on the fat of the land. Game there was in abundance, so much so, indeed, that they were a cause of anxiety, for the water in the vlei was decreasing rapidly from the number of animals that drank there nightly, and it was obvious that it would not last for very long unless rain fell. Signs were not wanting that the season had been exceptionally dry, for the vlei had at one time been of large extent, and now nothing but the one small pool remained. At it also drank myriads of partridges, the air being literally thick with the huge swarms of them that came in the early morning and again at night, so tame and fearless that they scarcely troubled to get out of our way, and we kept our pot going by simply knocking them over with a stick.

We soon explored the pan or oasis which was almost circular in shape and about a mile in diameter, and completely encircled by dunes; most of them as barren and forbidding as those we had already passed through, though to the south there was a certain amount of vegetation. This, however, was useless to us, as our way was east or north-east, and in this direction all Inyati's reconnoitering failed to discover anything but bare dunes, as far as the eye could reach.

Pleasant as the shade and greenery of the oasis was, it was evident that our stay could not be a lengthy one; moreover, lions were increasingly numerous, and for the first time in our trip began to cause us serious anxiety. So bold were they that fires had to be lit at nightfall and kept going all night; and their roars made sleep impossible.

The nights were now dark and moonless, and on the third of our stay the lions were exceptionally troublesome. We could see little beyond the light of the fires, but roars and growls came from all quarters, and there were evidences that a large herd of some kind of buck was passing through the oasis, and these the lions were attacking.

Inyati was nervous and uneasy, not, as he explained, on account of the lions, his "little gun" would see to them, but as to what was happening at the water-hole, from which we had removed our camp some distance on account of the lions.

"Gemsbok, master, a big herd of them, that is what it is," he said, as we listened to the terrific roars in the direction of the water. "They seek not water, for they seldom drink, but if it comes in their way they may do so; moreover, they will be likely to trample the pool into mud to cool their hooves. Luckily our water-skin is full, and the horses have drunk well; but I fear what the morning will show."

All night we could hear the buck moving about and passing through there must have been thousands of them. All night, too, the roaring continued, culminating shortly before daybreak with the most terrific uproar in the direction of the pool it was possible to imagine.

There the lions seemed to be making a combined attack, and judging by the sounds they were also fighting among themselves. As soon as it was daylight we hurried anxiously in that direction, keeping our rifles ready, although, as a rule, lions are little to be feared by daylight, unless disturbed at their meal. They were even more numerous than we had imagined, for huge dun-colored forms slunk off in all directions through the bush as we neared the water. "Water!" did I say? There was no water now, for Inyati's fears had been well-founded. The little pool had been trampled into black mud by countless gemsbok, and the various half-eaten carcasses strewn about showed that the lions had taken heavy toll of them.

Not without cost to themselves, however; for there in the centre of what had been the pool lay a huge lion, dead, transfixed and impaled upon the long, sharp, straight horns of the magnificent gemsbok bull, that lay, with broken neck, almost hidden beneath the lion's formidable bulk.

"Wow!" said Inyati; "I have heard of the like before. He was a strong bull, that old one, and held his horns straight to meet the lion's spring. And, as I feared, master, the water is gone."

It was obvious that nothing could be done with the black mud before us, for where it still remained moist it was full of blood and filth; and a decision thus forced upon us, we but waited till the power of the sun had somewhat abated before striking once more into the desert, due east. Our horses were rested and refreshed, and we pushed on throughout the night, till just before dawn we stumbled through a small patch of t'samma, and immediately decided to give our horses the benefit of them. Unfortunately, daylight showed the patch to be but a tiny one, where an arbitrary shower had fallen at the right season, and it barely sufficed for the day.

And so for days we pushed on incessantly, often going many miles out of our course to visit one of the many pans we now came across frequently, but failing in every case to find enough water to even replenish our water-skin. T'samma we found occasionally, sufficient, at any rate, to keep us and our animals alive, but barely; and the horrible anxiety of constant fear of a death by thirst had began to tell upon me badly. Not so Inyati, who, thirsty or satisfied, was always cheerful, always optimistic that we should eventually find a way through to his country of many diamonds and many wives! Many a weary trek that had landed us waterless and still further involved in the vast wilderness of dunes, had seen me sink despondent on the sand, caring but little whether I ever tried to struggle farther; to be roused from my lethargy by the cheery whimsicalities of this Micawber of the desert.

He would bring out the blue diamond and pretend to consult it as an oracle, and it would always promise him wonderful things! Sometimes for game was now scarce it would be a fat buck for breakfast; sometimes a vast plain of t'samma, or a big pool of water; and his prophecies always ended in unlimited diamonds and unlimited wives! And cheered by this nonsense, I would shake off the fit of despondency, and struggle on; though as time went on I often thought of Van der Decken, the "Flying Dutchman," and his endless effort to weather the Cape of Storms.

For our endless zigzagging in search of the wherewithal to live, though it had brought us to the very heart of the vast desert, had taken us far from the true direction of what we were in search of, nor could all our efforts find us a way through.

The moon was with us now again, and we trekked at night, seldom riding, but plodding doggedly through the endless succession of dunes, with the spiritless horses strung out behind us. Their hooves were splayed to an enormous size through this incessant trekking through the sand; yet, though broken and enfeebled, they had become more inured to the conditions, and the few t'samma, or tubers dug from the sand for them, sufficed to keep them alive.

I had ceased to take account of the time, but there came a day when we came upon a tract where rain had fallen in abundance some time before. For from an absolutely barren dune, we suddenly looked down upon a thick garden of beautiful flowers; tall, and like a slender foxglove in appearance, they filled the wide hollows between the dunes in all directions. They were of endless variety in color, white, mauve, and an endless gamut of pinks, down to the deepest purple; and a more beautiful sight it would be impossible to imagine. But thickly as they grew for mile after mile, there was nothing else, no t'samma or any other refreshing plant or fruit, and the hungry horses would not look at them. I noticed, too, that Inyati seemed none too pleased at finding this gorgeous garden, and climbed dune after dune to peer in all directions as the sun rose on the morning we found it.

"We must cross it quickly, or go round," he said, as I stood beside him on the top of a high dune. "It is a poison flower, and makes one sleep and to sleep among it is to die. But I see no way round!" Far on the horizon we could see the clouds rising from a pan in the right direction.

"We must go on," said Inyati, "and cross this belt of poison flower by day, when it will harm us but little; to be among it after sundown is to sleep and to sleep among it is to die."

I had heard of this poison flower before, but had never heard of its being found in such abundance as to be a danger to life. It looked too beautiful to be harmful, and its perfume was but faint. But Inyati knew it well, and I could see that he was anxious, as after a short rest we trekked on through the never-ending stretches of gorgeous coloring, through them, as through a cornfield. And soon I found that even now in the glaring sunshine when they were considered innocuous, their perfume had a peculiar effect upon me, and long before we had half crossed to the pan I was seized with an overpowering desire to sleep. I nodded as I stumbled along nothing seemed to matter why should we worry to go farther, why not lie down and rest, and sleep?

I must have stumbled and fallen, drugged with the insidious poison of the faint perfume, for I came to myself lying upon the ground among the flowers, and with Inyati shaking me violently and shouting in my ear. I was drunk with sleep, and it was with the utmost difficulty that he induced me to mount the only horse still capable of carrying me. We were parched with thirst, and our plight was perhaps worse than it had ever been, for all around stretched the fatal flowers, and it might well be that we could not clear them before night fell, and their poison became overpowering in its strength. On the horse, my head cleared somewhat, probably because I was higher from the ground, where the perfume hung heavily, although I could not rid myself of the drowsiness. At midday we were forced to halt for a rest forced, too, to take it in the glaring sun, on the top of a bare dune, for we dare not even cover ourselves with a bundle of the plants for fear of the poison. An hour or two we sat and grilled, and then forced ourselves onward once more, for the pan was still distant, and we feared we should not reach it before dark which would mean we would never reach it at all! But struggle as we would, we could make but little progress, and it was with mortal fear that I beheld the sun sink, and saw from a high dune that there was fully a mile of thick flowers between us and the pan, where dark bush and big trees showed plainly, and where the flowers ended abruptly.

"Let us stay here," I urged Inyati, "surely we are safe here on the top of the dune?" for we were fully fifty feet above the sea of flowers.

"No, master, no!" he answered emphatically; "if it were twice the height we should die before the night is out. Push through we must, even if we leave all our pack here and return for it tomorrow; and the horses must come too, or we shall lose them. Nothing could live here through the night." Hastily, as he spoke, he threw off the horses' already light loads, leaving everything but his beloved "little gun" on the top of the dune, and dragging the halter of the leading beast, he started down the slope. Instantly on entering the dense growth I felt the effect of the scent, which was now, although the sun had barely disappeared, ten times stronger than it had been in the sunlight. No faint sweetness now, but an overpowering scent similar to that of the well-known "moon-lilies" but infinitely stronger, and stupefying to a degree. Before fifty yards were traversed my head was spinning, and I was staggering like a drunken man. I remember Inyati half dragging me on to the horse again and feeling him lashing me to girth and saddle, remember his hoarse shouts to the horse and myself becoming fainter, remember dimly that the sjambok he flogged the horse with fell frequently across my back and legs, but nothing could keep me from the overwhelming desire to sleep And then all was a blank.

V - I LOSE INYATI

Water! Delicious cold water, being dashed in my face and trickling down my parched throat, brought me again to my senses. I lay, sore and bruised and with throbbing head and limbs, beside some tall reeds, between which water glittered in the light of the rising moon.

Inyati bent over me and he uttered an exclamation of joy as I opened my eyes.

"Master! master! I thought thee dead," he cried, "and surely would I then have died too! Right sorely did I beat thee, master, there among the devil flowers, to keep thee from the sleep that kills; but there was no one to beat me, and I had but strength and sense to tie myself too upon my horse before I too slept. And surely my sjambok must have helped them against the poison flowers, for they came right through, having smelt the water maybe; and brought us here to its very side, where I awoke to find them drinking. But the other is there in the dunes he will sleep well, that one; and die."

And die he did; for the next day, refreshed and fearing the flowers little in the day time, we went back to the dune where we had left our packs. It was barely a mile, and about half way we found the third horse, dead.

The pan was but a small one, and the delicious water of the night proved to be but a few gallons of stagnant liquid full of animalculae; but there was grass for the horses, and to our joy we found that the flower belt did not extend beyond where we had emerged from it. Bare dunes spread again beyond, but even these were welcome, after our experience of the "devil flowers," as Inyati called them. Buck was plentiful, and for a day or two we ate, drank, and slept to our heart's content, gathering all the strength we could for our next attempt. Inyati was full of confidence for the future, confident that we should never have difficulties to encounter equal to those we had surmounted, and that the diamonds and wives would soon be at our disposal.

"North, master! almost due north now and we shall find pans on the way with water! My magic stone has told me that and it makes no mistakes! And to-morrow we start again; for the water will last but a few days moreover, we have been long on the path."

Poor Inyati! the bravest, cheeriest comrade black or white that I have ever had; little did I dream when he spoke thus that he would never live to see the morrow!

That evening, as we sat smoking by the fire, we noticed that the two horses were extremely nervous, pricking their ears and snorting as they cropped the dry grasses a few yards away from us.

"Leopards," suggested Inyati, "there are many spoors here, but no lions."

But scarcely had he spoken when the booming roar of a lion came from the direction of the pool; to be immediately answered by another, and another; until it was evident that the pan had been invaded by a numerous troop of them. We both started to our feet with the same thought in our minds. If they were hungry they might probably attack the horses! It was still light, but no time was to be lost; so hastily cutting down a number of the stunted thorn bushes with which the pan abounded, we proceeded to build a "scherm" in which to pass the night.

We enclosed a space about fifteen yards square, and into this we brought the horses, together with enough wood to keep a fire burning all night; and as the hedge was seven or eight feet in height, and of impenetrable thorn, we felt but little anxiety as to the presence of the lions. As night fell, however, their roars became louder and nearer, and by mid-night there were at least a dozen of them pacing round our scherm, and barely kept at a distance by the frequent fire- brands we threw over the fragile protection. Occasionally the huge beasts fought amongst themselves, and the snarling, growling pandemonium would become more deafening; then this diversion would cease, and the whole troop would continue their pacing round our fence, sniffing and snorting at us through the thorn bushes and making us feel as one can imagine a mouse feels when caught in a trap, and with a hungry cat peering through the bars at him. Time after time we scared them away by throwing fire-brands among them, but always they returned, and to our dismay, long before morning we realized that our stock of firewood would not nearly last till daylight.

We had refrained from shooting, as it was impossible to see the brutes through our scherm; but as the fire got lower, and they became more daring, we sent a few shots among them, and the hellish hubbub that ensued showed that some of them were hit. But this proved disastrous, for a wounded animal, in its death struggles near the fence, came in contact with the bushes and almost tore down our only protection before a few more bullets finished it. There came a lull for a short time after this, and we were congratulating ourselves that morning would soon be dawning, when the lions would slink away, or when the light would enable us to finish them when without the least warning a huge form leapt clean over the hedge and landed in the centre of the scherm, scattering the few remaining embers in all directions.

A second spring, and before either of us could shoot, the lion had pounced upon Inyati, and had him down upon the ground beneath him, shaking the poor fellow like a terrier shakes a rat. Mad with rage I sent bullet after bullet into the brute's head and body till the click of the hammer of my Winchester showed the magazine was empty, and the lion rolled over dead, with Inyati still in its mighty grip, and to all appearance dead also.

Then I must have gone berserk mad. I remember cramming the magazine full again, and throwing aside the bush that blocked the entrance, I stepped out among the lions.

I can never understand why I was not killed instantly; but not a lion reached me, and at close range I fired shot after shot in the bright moonlight, and lion after lion fell, till but two were left; and as morning dawned these slunk away, leaving me alone with my dead.

Then I came back to the scherm, my mad fit of rage over, and nothing but grief, and a sorrow too deep for words to express, left in my heart. The huge lion lay right across the poor boy's body, still gripping his crushed shoulder in its mighty jaws; but now I saw that in spite of his terrible injuries Inyati was not dead, though he was dying even as I came back to him. Strong as I was, no strength of mine could have freed him from the grip of those terrible jaws, and as I struggled to do so, his beseeching glance stopped me. I knelt down beside him.

"Finished, master! finished," he whispered, "yet we have made a good fight and you, master, will win. Straight north now! Bury the little gun with me, master. It may serve me who knows? And take thou the blue stone, and this my armlet, it may help . . . master, master, I go. . . ."

And with his eyes fixed upon me, he died; that brave heart, that had served me so well.

I was stupefied with the blow that had fallen upon me, and lay for an hour or more as one stunned.

Once or twice the craven thought came upon me to use a bullet to end it all, and once I actually lifted my revolver to my head; but dead Inyati's last whisper seemed again to sound in my ear had I made a "good fight," to end it like a coward?

And so I lay in the shade of a tree, and sleep, the blessed healer, came to me and saved my reason. For when I awoke, although my heart was heavy, my brain was clear, and I knew what lay before me, and no longer shirked the task.

The lion's head I hewed from its body, for I could not tear its huge jaws asunder to release Inyati, and there I buried victim and victor together.

And so, I was alone, in the heart of the desert, with return an impossibility.

I struck north, as Inyati had told me, due north; in spite of the fact that in that direction the dunes were of the worst; and for a day, and half a night, I wayfared, striving in sheer physical suffering to drown the sorrow of losing Inyati. God knows what I went through, or the poor horses that I drove ruthlessly forward; moreover, the fever that was already burning in my veins may have rendered me delirious? Certain it is that this part, and many a day afterwards, is but a confused dream to me. A dream of suffering, of incessant wandering from pan to pan; here a few mouthfuls of stagnant water, and there a few t'samma still keeping myself and the horses alive. For days the wandering must have been purely mechanical: but one day I came to myself just as the sun was setting. I felt weak and exhausted but perfectly sane. I was parched, and my water-skin was gone, probably thrown away in a fit of frenzy or despair I could not remember.

The horses, mere wrecks of what they had been, were munching the last of a small patch of t'samma; and I was barely in time to rescue a couple of still eatable ones, to moisten my parched tongue.

I had no idea how long I had been lying there unconscious, but the idea of pushing north had now become an obsession with me, and I staggered to the highest dune to look around me. I was still in a wilderness of dunes, but I noticed that what little vegetation there was, was new and strange to me; indeed, except for the t'samma there was scarce a bush or plant I could recognize.

It was evident that I had traveled far in my delirium, and my heart bounded, as I made out, away to the north, a kopje of rugged rocks rising from the dunes. Here, apparently, then, I was at length reaching the confines of this wilderness of sand, for these were the first rocks that I had seen since we entered the desert it seemed a lifetime back!

The kopje was in the right direction too, for Inyati had said "keep north" and by reaching it I should at least be able to spy out the land.

I lost no time in saddling up, finding that I had still a small amount of biltong and plenty of ammunition left. Nearly all night I trekked through barren dunes, but these were now small and easy to traverse compared to the mountains of sand I had already passed through, and when I lay down for an hour before dawn I felt sure daylight would show me to be near the kopje. Such was the case, for I found myself barely a mile from it, and soon had reached its bare and boulder-strewn base. It was perhaps three hundred feet high, of bare granite boulders heaped one on the other, with big cavities between them, and all so rounded and smooth that I had great difficulty in climbing it, but at length I stood on the huge boulder poised on the summit. And from it, to my joy, I saw glimmering away on the far northern horizon a wide stretch of water. I rubbed my eyes and peered again and again, for often the false mirage had raised my hopes to a frantic pitch by its glittering deception. But this was water, and I could scarce refrain from setting forth immediately in its direction, yet, knowing the exhausted state of the horses I feared to do so, and seeking a hollow under a gigantic boulder I lay through the heat of that long scorching day, parched and longing for the water I had seen, dreaming of it when I dozed, and gloating over it when awake. How I would revel in it; could I ever be satisfied again to do aught but drink, and drink, and lay and soak my sun-scorched body in it, and drink again?

Impatient as I was, the day seemed intolerably long, but at length the sun was sufficiently low to allow of the horses trekking again, although the poor beasts' plight was pitiful. Again I trekked through the better part of the night, due north, and with no fear of missing the water, for it was a wide sheet that the kopje had shown me almost a lake it appeared to be.

Towards morning the horses were so exhausted that I could scarcely urge them forward, and I myself but stumbled doggedly on, kept alive solely by the knowledge that soon now I should drink.

And now, thank God, I could see the water faintly reflecting the light in the east, and just as the sun rose I stumbled clear of the dunes. Before me stretched a wide sheet of water, several miles in length, the shores barren and destitute of vegetation, and without a sign of bird or animal life. My heart mis-gave me, as I noticed how silent, dead, and forbidding the place was: noticed, too, that the horses made no attempt to reach the water they were dying for, but stood dejected and spirit-less where I had let go of their bridles. A few staggering strides and my awful doubt was confirmed. For the water was as salt as brine!

And now for a time I gave way to absolute despair. I was exhausted, and tortured by thirst, my lips cracked and swollen, my tongue like leather; and I felt that when the sun reached its full power I must perish in the horrible agony and madness of a death from thirst unless indeed my revolver saved me the last torture! Sorely was I tempted, as I lay there by the brink of the salt lake, where I had thrown myself down in the agony of my disappointment.

But, thank God, I kept my sanity, and even in that terrible plight Hope again crept into my heart.

"T'samma!" There might be t'samma there to the right where the dunes were higher, and the sand redder, certainly a little dark vegetation appeared to show in the hollows.

And so I staggered to my feet again, and leaving the horses I made my panting, laborious way across to the dunes I had marked, on the eastern shore of the lake. They were about half a mile away, and it seemed as though I should never reach them, but at length I entered the hollow between two of them, and found a few stunted bushes covered with red berries the size of cherries, and the like of which I had never seen before. I hesitated to eat them, for many of the desert berries are poisonous, and almost all are bitter and acrid, but I could see no t'samma, and so I bit one, hesitatingly at first, but as the sharp, delicious flavor penetrated my scorched palate, ravenously.

Cool, full of juice, and of a flavor something like a black-currant, they tasted to me the most delicious morsel that had ever passed my lips, and all thoughts of their being poison left me, as I plucked and ate them greedily. Most grateful they were, and soon I felt a new being, though some poisonous properties they must have contained, for within a few minutes I felt a rush of blood to my head, a buzzing in my ears, and was soon staggering as though drunk. I ate no more then, and in a short time the effects passed off, and wonderfully refreshed and invigorated, I made my way back to the horses; who, the image of despair, stood where I had left them.

I literally dragged them to the little bushes, which to my delight they ate greedily; fruit, foliage, and even the bare twigs. So, again I was respited; but I knew it to be only a respite, for the bushes were few, and I could find no sign of others or of t'samma.

And so for days I wandered, finding a few of the berries here and there, often half maddened and stupefied by them, my head awhirl too with fever, alternately hoping and despairing, my sense of direction almost gone, striving, whenever possible, to work north in my lucid moments, but finding often by crossing my own spoor that I had been wandering in a vain circle.

Then one afternoon, as I lay in a sort of semi-stupor beneath one of the bushes that had yielded me a fair number of berries, a sharp gust of wind aroused me, and looking around me I saw, whirling across the bare dunes towards me, a huge cloud of thick opaque dust, gathering up the loose sand as it sped, whirling high in the air and blotting out the whole sky with its dense volume, snatching up, carrying away, and burying deep again, all that came in its path. It was a sandstorm, and I was in its path, here amongst the loose dunes, where escape seemed impossible. I must fly or be buried! The horses, snorting with fear, would have bolted had I not caught them quickly; and tired as they were, they needed no urging on from the destroying monster that sped relentlessly after them. The dunes were here low and open, and the red berries on which the horses had lived of late, seemed to have maddened and stimulated them, for they seemed to fly on the very wings of the wind. Right before the storm they sped, the first advance gusts eddying around us, the sky overhead already thick with the flying sand.

And now, maddened with fever, intoxicated with the strange stimulation of the berries I too had been eating, I no longer fled in fear, but in its place came a wild exhilaration, and I shouted aloud as I flogged the panting horses to further efforts.

Now, to my disordered brain, the sandstorm was a legion of pursuing fiends, that snatched at me from every gust and eddy; now, too, they were gaining on us, and I shrieked and fought with the imaginary demons as, in spite of the speed of the horses, the storm gained on us and enveloped us more and more at every stride. And so for an eternity I seemed to fly, now hemmed in with blinding sand, seeing nothing, knowing nothing but an overpowering desire to escape from the clutching fiends around, tortured with thirst maddened, screaming. Dark now, as at midnight, except when a flash of forked lightning burst through the driving chaos; now I had burst free again, as the storm veered in another direction, yet still it threatened me and still I galloped on. Then a snort of fright from the horses, a wild plunge forward that almost threw me from the saddle, a sense of falling, a stunning crash that seemed to me to be the bursting asunder of the world's very foundations and then a merciful oblivion.

VI - THE CRATER THE PLEASANT BERRIES SLEEP AND THE AWAKENING

I awoke to the tortures of the damned, crushed, broken and in agonizing pain, and with the aasvogels tearing at my face. Pinned to the earth as by some great weight, my hands were fortunately still free; and my revolver still in its holster; and a few shots sent the lewd, cowardly birds flapping away. The blood was streaming from my face, and again and again I fainted with sheer agony; moreover the fierce midday sun beat down intolerably full in my eyes, for I lay on my back and could move nothing but my arms. But gradually the sun passed, a cool shadow fell across me, and although I believed I was hurt unto death and indeed longed for death to end my agony some modicum of relief must have come with the shade, and with it strength and the desire to live. Moreover, it was borne upon me that from somewhere near me came the sound of running, gurgling water; tantalizing and maddening me in my pain and agony. I was lying on a slope with my head lower than my limbs, and all I could see was the sky above me; do all I could, I could not lift myself, and could not see what pinned my lower limbs to the sand.

But, maddened more, I believe, by thirst and hearing water running, than by the actual agony of my hurt, I at length began to work at the sand on either side of me with my hands, scratching it away until I had altered my position enough to enable me to turn somewhat, and raise myself a little on one elbow.

Then I found it was my dead horses that pinned me down, for both of them lay crushed and broken partly above me; and looking upwards I saw that a sheer cliff of smooth rock towered straight above me, from which the horses had evidently fallen.

I could hear the water plainer now, and though I swooned once or twice from agony, I gradually worked my limbs clear of the incubus pressing on them, and tried to stand up. But this I could not do, some injury to my spine preventing me, and it was as a beast, on all fours, that I at length made shift to crawl in search of the water I was dying for. Each yard I crawled was agony to me, but at last I came to a rock-encircled pool in which lay water clear and deep, and into which a tiny stream splashed and gurgled from an overhanging cliff. Sweet and pure the water was, and in great abundance. I peered into its dark depths and could see the white sand glimmering at the bottom, full ten or twelve feet below me as I judged.

I crawled to it, and I drank as I had never drank before; and I bathed my tortured face and limbs; finding that, miraculously, none were broken, though I was bruised and aching in every bone, and to stand erect was quite beyond me.

So I drank, and slept, and drank again, and later found strength and appetite sufficient to crawl back to where the dead horses lay, and to search among the scattered contents of my pack for some biltong, and the wherewithal to dress my wounds.

And thus for days I lived, and nursed myself gradually back to a measure of my former strength; dragging myself painfully from the water to the shadow of the rocks to sleep, feeling little anxiety as to where I was or what was to happen to me. I had water in plenty and food sufficient for the present, and after the awful experiences of the desert my one desire was to rest and sleep.

But with returning health came curiosity; and although I was still bent and could not walk upright, I managed to move about and to find out something of this strange prison into which I had been hurled in my frantic flight before the sandstorm.

Apparently I was in the hollow cup of an extinct crater, for on all sides towered perpendicular cliffs of dark granite-like rock, so smooth and unbroken for the most part that a baboon would scarce have found foothold upon them indeed, in many places they actually overhung. Almost circular, and about a quarter of a mile in diameter, the floor of this place was to a great extent covered in verdure, broken here and there with rocks, and except where I had fallen there was but little bare sand.

How I had escaped being smashed to pieces was inexplicable, for the sheer wall of rock that penned me in was, I judged, at least five hundred feet in height, and the horses' bones now picked clean by the aasvogels had been smashed by the terrible fall. A short examination of my little domain showed me that although escape from it was apparently hopeless especially in my maimed condition there was no need for me to starve, and indeed my prison was a very pleasant one. There were wild fruits in abundance, many of them unknown to me, but prominent among them the red, luscious, intoxicating berries that had saved my life in the desert; and these I now ate greedily, finding them much riper than when I had first tasted them, and their effect much more potent. They intoxicated me, perhaps maddened me, and dulled my intellect for the time; but they gave respite to my pain-racked frame, and gave me sleep. Sometimes for days I would give myself up to them, eating nothing else, and lying in a pleasant, dreamy stupor by the deep pool, staring into the dark, clear depths where the white sand glimmered so white.

At times I roused myself sufficiently to search for other food, of which there was plenty. Partridges and other fowl swarmed at the water, and were easily killed or trapped, and there was plenty of t'samma growing quite close to the spot where I had fallen.

These, since I had now an abundance of water, I did not attempt to eat; taking only the pips from the ripe ones, drying them in the sun, and pounding them between two stones, as I had often seen the Bushmen do. From the coarse meal thus obtained I made little cakes, roasting them on hot stones or the embers of my fire. Matches I had none, but my burning glass served me just as well, for every day the sun shone; indeed seldom did a cloud cross the sky, and whatever storms may have raged outside nothing but the gentlest breeze ever reached the deep hollow that held me a willing prisoner. Willing? Well, at least apathetic; for all hope, all ambition, all interest in life had left me. I had forgotten the reason of my quest, forgotten the girl who had sent me on it, forgotten that I was once an erect and vigorous man with other interests than to crawl round for berries like an ape, and lie all day and sleep when once hunger was appeased. And thus I led an invertebrate, purposeless existence. I had warmth, food, and water, and the berries that gave me pleasant dreams, and I wanted nothing more. I took no note of the passing of time weeks, months God knows? even years! may have passed nay must have passed as in a dream, and I might well have died there beside the long-bleached skeletons of my horses, but that one day chance or fate led me back to the path of reason. I had been sleeping off the effects of the berries, and lay, beneath the shade of a rock close to the pool, idly tossing about the tiny pebbles of the little patch of shingle close to its brink playing with them as a child might. And suddenly a glint on the corner of one of these little stones arrested my wandering attention; there was something familiar about it, something that stirred memories in my sluggish brain. What was it? I groped in vain for some clue. The pebble worried me, and I made a peevish gesture to throw it away. No! Whatever it was, I must not do that, rather wash it, wash it. Yes! that was what we used to do. But where was the batea, for now by some strange freak I was back in Brazil, and must have my batea. We washed our gravel for diamonds in that wooden prospecting pan--diamonds?

My mind was stirring troubling me now, and with a trembling hand I thrust the pebble into a handful of others and worked them between my palms in the water. Yes, there it was, a good stone of ten carats-- slightly encrusted with oxide--a good find. And I? Where was I?

I stood gazing alternately at the stone, and at my surroundings: the pool, the circle of towering cliffs that hemmed me in, and gradually the flood-gates of my clouded memory broke loose and I remembered all.

The girl in England, old Anderson, Inyati, and the blue diamond; my ride and fall; all these came back to me almost in a flash, stunning and amazing me; but for long the incidents of my life here in the hollow were vague and misty. The berries! Surely they had been the cause of my lethargy, and even as I thought of them the desire for them came upon me. But for the first time I fought it, for in my reawakened brain other desires were now surging.

Diamonds! Inyati had told me there were plenty in his land; had Fate with a cruel irony led me into this land of wealth only to maim me and keep me a lonely prisoner here in this pit till I died!

All this flashed through my mind as I stood and gazed at the stone; then, righting my inclination for the berries, I plunged into the pool, and found new strength and resolution in its refreshing coolness. Then I searched eagerly amongst the other pebbles and found three more diamonds, all fine big stones; yet not to be compared with the blue stone Inyati had given me. Where was it? My pack had been scattered by that terrific fall, but now I remembered the diamond had been sewn securely into the cartridge belt I had always worn. It must be here now with my clothes.

For now I realized that I was naked as a savage clothed but in the long tangled hair on head and chin scarred, blistered and burnt till I looked like a wild man, as I had indeed become.

And then I remembered my face, the vultures! and looking into the clear waters of the pool, I saw, for the first time with sane eyes, my terrible disfigurement, and cried aloud in anguish as I saw what manner of man I had become, and realized that even if I could escape life was for me a closed book. Scarred, grotesque, and horrible; what future was there for me among my fellow beings . . . even though I could return to them? Again I was sorely tempted to seek the berries that would give me oblivion from all this agony of regret; but I struggled, and as night came I slept a natural, refreshing sleep, and awoke with a new-born hope and determination strong in me. I would not die here as a wild beast; some-how I would scale the cliffs and escape, or die in the attempt a better death than to perish like a rat in a trap without a struggle for liberty.

My head was clearer now than it had been for I know not how long, and I could reason. And Inyati's diamond was my first thought. I could find but little trace of my pack; the white bones of my horses were half buried in sand; a rusty tin here and a few shreds of clothing there being all that I could find near them. My rifle I found; or rather the remnants of it, for it had been broken to pieces in the fall, and no trace of the stock remained. At length in a crevice near the pool I found my revolver with a number of cartridges, my hunting knife, and a few odds and ends of clothing, all in a canvas haversack that still remained strong and sound, and at the bottom my belt and the diamond tied up with Inyati's brace-let. But the leather belt had perished to a remarkable degree; it was hard, black, cracked and twisted, and broke at my first touch; and I found too upon searching for the saddles that nothing remained of them but some dried fragments. I realized then that months must have passed since my fall; but even then I had no conception of the terrible truth! Cheered by the discovery of the blue diamond, I now determined to look closely for others in the vicinity of the pool, but days of laborious search-ing brought no reward except that the work helped more and more to clear my foggy brain and bring me back to full sanity. I felt convinced that diamonds were there, not far off, however, and one day as I vainly sorted over the gravel where I had found the others, the solution came to me. In the pool, in the white sand that shone so at the bottom, there I should find them! It was deep and narrow, this pool, and a difficult task even for a good diver; and I determined to wait till midday, when the sun shone full on the bottom. When the time came I plunged in, and a rapid stroke or two took me to the bottom.

The water was clear as crystal; and now I could see clearly why it had looked so white and sparkled so when seen through the rippling surface.

Stretched upon the white sand lay the chalk-white skeleton of a man, the grinning mouth and sightless eyes staring up at me in a hideous travesty of mirth; and all around between the outstretched bones lay diamonds, diamonds innumerable: big, bright, sparkling beauties by the handful, wealth incredible to be had for the picking up, with no guardian other than these bare bones of a long dead man.

The shock of coming face to face with this grim "memento mori" here in the depths of the pool was too much even for my desire for the diamonds, and I struck frantically for the surface, clambering out in wild, senseless, unreasoning fear, and not even pausing till I was well away from the vicinity of this spot, which had been my favorite resting place for so long. And that night I tried in vain to sleep, my brain whirling with wild surmises, as to how the long-dead man had found his way into the crater. Was there a path after all, or had he used a rope to let himself down in search of the diamonds, only to meet his death in some manner where they lay thickest?

Or had he, perchance, passed years in the trap, vainly endeavoring to find a way out, pacing day after day round the ring of encircling cliffs, until at last, in utter despair, he had thrown himself into the pool to end it all, and to leave his bones there watching the treasure he could not take with him?

Each time I closed my eyes the mocking, grinning skeleton seemed to be again before me, and it was not till early morning that I could rest. But with the day my fears vanished; indeed what was there to fear, for how could these few poor bones harm me?

Still, I could not bring myself to dive into the pool again, but set about devising some other means of getting the diamonds. An empty gourd, cut into the shape of a bowl, and lashed to a stick, solved the difficulty, and with this primitive dredge I brought up diamonds sufficient for a king's ransom; so many indeed that long before night even I was satisfied. Large lustrous stones they were, of splendid water, and several of them were blue, though none were as fine as the one Inyati had given me. ...

So here was wealth far beyond my wildest dreams, and if I could but escape then, even disfigured as I was, life might still hold pleasures for me.

Even if the girl who had sent me to this turned away in horror from my hideous disfigurements, there was much that money could bring travel, adventure, sport, a thousand things and, at any rate, the companionship of rational beings, for which I now craved as I had craved for water in the desert. For God knows how long I had seen no human being no living creature indeed but a few birds and I had almost forgotten the sound of a human voice. Sunk in apathy I had become almost as a beast, but the sight of the diamonds had aroused me, and I recalled how poor Inyati had called them "magic stones." Magic indeed, for they had saved my reason.

And with the sight of all this wealth the desire to escape grew stronger, and with it grew a hatred of my hitherto pleasant prison until the thought of remaining in it became intolerable to me. That very evening I began a minute examination of my prison walls; but it was not till several days had passed that I at length discovered a route where here a crack, there a tiny ledge, and again a small projection, offered a precarious chance of foot or hand-hold, and where, if anywhere at all, a human being might essay the terrible climb to the desert above, with a remote chance of success. My mind made up on this point, I made what preparation I could for the climb, and for the desert beyond it. My water bottle was still sound, and little as it held it must suffice. For food I killed a number of the partridges and roasted them, cutting away their plump breasts from the bone, for I realized that in the terrible climb before me every ounce would tell; my knife, revolver, and a few cartridges I made a belt for by plaiting the strong coarse grass that grew near the water, and of the same material I made a hat, for I remembered, only too well, that I should find no shade in the desert should I succeed in my desperate attempt.

Shoes I had none, but this did not trouble me, for my feet were hardened to the consistency of leather. The diamonds I made into a bundle with some shreds of clothing, and stowed them in the canvas haversack, except for Inyati's and a few other blue ones which I luckily put in my pocket.

All these belongings I conveyed one evening to the foot of the cliff up which I intended attempting to climb, sleeping at the spot so as to be ready and fresh for a start at daybreak. I feared little as to my strength, for in spite of my injuries I was now stronger than I had ever been; but what I did fear was vertigo. From a child I had always had a horror of looking down from a great height, feeling an almost irresistible desire to throw myself down whenever I did so, and I feared that as I neared the top this would happen and I should be dashed again to the floor of the crater.

But better that and death than this endless captivity; and I did not shrink from my formidable undertaking. At early dawn I drank deep from the gushing water that I was leaving, and fastening on my load I began to climb. For a time all went well, though of necessity my progress was but slow, and the sun was full overhead when I halted for a rest on a small ledge about half way up. Here for the first time since I started I could lie at full length without having to hold on, and I needed the rest, for the strain had been terrific, and I feared that the worst part of the climb was still to come.

So far, I had resisted all inclination to look down, but shortly after leaving the ledge I was compelled to do so. I had been following a crack running diagonally up from it, and which from below had appeared to connect with another ledge favorable to me, but to my consternation I found that this was not the case, ten or twelve feet of absolutely smooth and vertical rock cutting me off from my coveted path to freedom. I was flattened against the wall, my heels overhanging the abyss, clutching with one hand a projection above me, and feeling with my other for a new grip; but the rock was as smooth as polished marble, and it was evident that I must work back to the ledge I had rested on and try for a new route. And to do this I had of necessity to look down. As I did so the deadly vertigo I feared so much came over me, and it was well that I had good hand and foothold, or I should certainly have fallen. As it was I clung helpless, sick, and giddy, with closed eyes for some time, and it was only by the strongest effort of my will that I could force myself to again open them, and work my way gradually back to the little ledge. There I threw myself down, panting and deadly sick, the whole world seeming to spin round me; and there I lay for some time inert and helpless, before I could brace myself sufficiently for a further effort. At length I roused myself and started up again in another direction, towards where I could see a few stunted bushes growing, and here to my joy I found a wider ledge than the last, leading steeply upwards. It came to an end, however, far below the cliff top; moreover, at this part the top actually overhung me, and it was evident I must attempt to work my way farther round before climbing higher. To add to my anxiety I noticed now that evening was fast approaching and I realized that I had but little daylight left to me, and should darkness find me still clinging like a fly to the face of the cliff my fate was certain. I was almost exhausted, and my heart sank as I searched in vain for a way up. The distance was not great now, a bare fifty feet separating me from the topmost pinnacle, but though I walked along the bottom of this barrier for some distance it still presented the same insurmountable difficulties.

And the sun had set, and dusk was already falling, when half frantic with fear, I at length made out a crevice which appeared to offer a possible means of saving my life. It ran diagonally across the rock at a steep angle upwards, going out of my sight around a big buttress that overhung me, and I could not tell whether it reached to the actual top or not. But it was my only chance, and with my heart in my mouth I made my way towards it. I could just reach it, and setting my teeth and summoning all my courage, I gripped it fast and made my way gradually upward. For a few yards my feet found a little foothold to help me, but soon I was dangling over the awful abyss. I dare not think of what lay below me, but with set teeth, and muscles cracking with the strain, I edged gradually along till I rounded the buttress face, and here within ten feet of the summit I found scanty foothold again. Here I stood quivering and exhausted till I had regained my breath, and then in the fast waning light I examined the few feet of rock that still stood between me and freedom. Barely two feet above my outstretched hand was the pinnacle that formed the edge of the cliff, but how was I to reach it? To spring from my precarious foothold was impossible, and not the slightest hold could I find for my fingers anywhere to draw myself up. Night was now upon me, to return to the ledge was out of the question, and I knew that I could not cling for long where I was, but that long before daylight came again I must fall into the awful abyss that yawned beneath me. God! to die like this after all my struggle, to die within a few inches of freedom. Had I but a rope! And with the thought came inspiration. The sling of the haversack! It was of stout, strong canvas, and might hold could I but throw the loop over the pinnacle. It was a poor chance but my only one. Hastily slipping it off I held the bag in my right hand, and clutching my only handhold with the left, I attempted to throw the loop over the sharp point above me. Again and again I missed, and it was in an agony of despair, when, at last, it fell clear over the point and held. I hauled at it with all the strength of my free arm and it held firm. But would it hold my weight? This I could not test, but I must perforce stake all upon the chance, for there was no other chance. Should a strand of the canvas give, down I must go hurtling to my death. There was no other way, and with an inarticulate prayer I gripped the strap fast with my other hand and swung myself upwards. A second later although in my agony it seemed an eternity and my hand clutched the pinnacle itself; a wild convulsive scramble and I was up safe . . . and free . . at last! And even as I dragged myself into freedom, the haversack, loosened from its hold, fell with all its precious contents into the black depths below!

VII - THE COUNTRY OF CRATERS, THE PATH OF SKULLS, AND THE SNAKE

Filled, as I could but be, with thankfulness at my escape from captivity and from an awful death, I did not realize for a time what the loss of the diamonds meant to me; indeed I was too exhausted by my terrific struggle to do more than crawl a few yards away from the brink, throw myself down in the sand and sink into the sleep of utter weariness.

But with my awakening the bitter truth was borne upon me in a flash. All my struggle had then been in vain. I had won my freedom but had lost all that would make life bearable. Even if I could win back through the desert, what had I now to compensate me for the horrible disfigurement that would make me shunned and despised a leper amongst my fellowmen?

Bitterly did I regret my pleasant prison down below surely it would have been better to stay there in peace till I died, as fate had apparently decreed; and if I could have done so I would certainly have returned. But to return was impossible, and I must make up my mind to struggle through the desert or die where I was. Moreover, in the midst of my bitter reflections there came the comforting recollection that I had still the blue diamonds that I had kept apart and put in my pocket. Eagerly I felt for them yes! they were safe, and in themselves they must be worth a fortune!

My spirits rose with a bound again; why should I dream of giving in? I was strong and hard, and if I could win through, the diamonds would surely enable me to fit out an expedition and return; and with ropes the descent into the crater would be easy.

Rested by the cool of the night I felt little the worse for my climb, and was all eagerness for dawn to break that I might see what manner of country I was in, for I had been half demented when my terrible ride from the pursuing sandstorm had brought me into it.

At last daylight came, and I saw that although in the midst of a wide sandy plain, there were no dunes; scattered bushes grew here and there, and dotted about in the distance were a number of bare granite rocks. The crater I had climbed from went sheer down at my feet so abruptly indeed, and with so little to denote its presence, that within a few yards of its brink nothing whatever could be seen of it.

I looked once more into its depths, to where the pool lay dark in the still dim light of dawn, and from it my eyes followed the course that I had taken in my climb, and I marveled that I had ever reached the top. And a great thankfulness rose in my heart and drowned the unworthy regret that I had felt at the loss of the diamonds.

And with a last long look at my late prison, I turned and made my way towards a prominent pile of rocks in the distance, from which I hoped to be able to see more of my surroundings. My waterbottle was nearly empty already, and the old haunting dread of thirst was beginning to fill my mind, but soon this fear left me, for within a mile I found t'samma flourishing, and at the first pile of rocks a little spring of water.

Cheered and encouraged I made good progress in spite of the now blazing sun, and soon I reached the pile of rocks. And to my astonishment I found that they formed part of the margin of a crater almost identical with the one from which I had escaped; deep and inaccessible, and with a mass of vegetation filling the bottom.

This discovery gave me food for thought. It had never entered my head that the queer place of my imprisonment had been one of many, and I had thought that once I could reach even a friendly native tribe where some kind of rope was obtainable I could locate the crater again and secure the bag of diamonds. But I had already stumbled upon another crater, and maybe there were many? And this indeed I found to be the case, for they became more numerous as I proceeded, until the whole country was pitted with them. They were of all sizes and depths, some mere pits of fifty feet in diameter or less, some huge gulfs a mile or more across, and so deep that it was difficult to distinguish what was at the bottom. Invariably their walls were sheer and I could explore none of them, but in nearly all I saw the gleam of water.

So numerous were they, as I penetrated farther into this strange country, that I was forced to make wide detours in my endeavor to avoid them, and so bewildering did this labyrinth of huge pits at last become that I became hopelessly lost among them, and at times thought that I should never break clear of them again. Day after day I wandered about this vast and apparently level plain, finding every short distance a huge yawning gulf at my feet, forced to try new routes, and constantly being pulled up by similar obstacles. And all this time I saw no sign of life, not even a spoor in the sand to show that mankind had ever trod there. There was no animal life even; a few birds, and a few snakes, nothing more indeed so deserted and dead was this weird land that it appeared unreal, and often I imagined that by some strange chance I had been transported to some other and long-dead planet, so little was this maze of craters like Mother Earth.

I had food and water enough, and as the moon now gave plenty of light I walked only at night, resting in the shadow of the rocks by day.

One night I had made better progress than usual, having walked for some hours without having to deviate from my path, and was beginning to hope that I had escaped from the labyrinth, when suddenly, at my very feet, there yawned the usual abyss, but this time so huge that I could scarce make out the farther cliffs, though the moon was full and it was almost as light as day. It would mean a long and weary detour, and my heart sank as I thought of it; then leapt as it had not leapt since the day I found the diamond by the pool in the crater. For there in the misty depths, far away towards the farther cliffs, twinkled a fire!

A fire! Yes; and I had seen no fire except of my own kindling since the night that Inyati had died . . . months months surely it must have been years ago? . . .

Here at last must be human beings: savages maybe, but still flesh and blood like myself; and if they were in the crater there must be a way down.

That night I walked as I had never walked before, following the brink of the chasm, and scarcely taking my eyes from the tiny flame that meant so much to me. A way out, a way back to civilization, to life among beings like myself, all this it would mean to me, even if I found but savages by the fire for they could put me in the right path . . . and it never occurred to me to fear them.

Now as the broad moon rose higher I could see into the crater's depths, and this, besides being more vast, was not as the others I had seen. Its floor appeared to be quite level, and looked to be of pure white sand; but everywhere it sparkled in the bright moonlight. Diamonds surely?

I was near the fire now, though far above it, and now I could see there was a path, a broad white path, down a steep slope, it must be broad to show so plainly, for I was still a mile or more away!

In my eagerness I forgot my fatigue, and hastened panting towards this first blessed sign of man's handiwork that I had seen for so long.

Here it was at last; a broad white road, running straight as an arrow away across the sands in the one direction and leading down into the pit on the other a road paved apparently with round white stones all of one size.

Something in their appearance struck me: a loose one lay beside the path, and I stooped to examine it.

It was a skull a human skull, the whole road was paved with them as far as the eye could reach, there were thousands upon thousands myriads of them.

And as I realized what they were, fear seized me, and I turned away from this terrible pathway.

At last I threw myself down in the black shadow of some rocks, still trembling and agitated, and tried to compose myself to think. What manner of men were these I had found at last, and who watched there below by the fire: what race was this that thus made grim mockery of their dead?

At length I overcame my fears sufficiently to return not to the path but to the edge of the crater at some distance from it, and peering down could see that the fire was still burning, and here, hiding as best I could, I waited till morning. Daylight showed me no sign of life however, though still the pale flame flickered, and I could now make out that it burnt before a sort of building which seemed to be of white polished stone. Till well after broad daylight I lay and watched, but nothing stirred; and I determined that I would go down and see what manner of fire was this that burnt day and night without tending.

The skulls did not look as ghastly in sunlight as they had done in the pale light of the moon. I could see too that this path was ancient, and nowhere could I find traces of its being used. As I had seen the night before, it led straight across the desert, and in the distance in that direction I could now see faint blue mountains. So there was an end to this land of desolation after all, and I determined that after I had seen what was below, I would follow that road! The slope went down steeply and here the path was roughly stepped; as it led deeper, too, the slope narrowed, until at the bottom the entrance to the crater lay through a natural gateway of rock that rose high on either hand and almost shut out the light. Through it the strange path led, and here in the gloom the horror of this awful place again came upon me and I could scarce bring myself to enter the narrow defile. I remember clutching my revolver as I went forward at last: remember thinking too that it could avail me nothing, for here was no live being to fear, here was naught but the dead. . The utter silence and loneliness even after my months of silence and loneliness seemed to weigh upon me like a heavy burden, and when a bat came fluttering by me in the gloom I uttered a hoarse cry of alarm. But the distance was but short, and soon I stood safe in the daylight again, and on the floor of the crater. And now I could see that the white floor I had thought was sand was also strewn with bones, of animals principally, though men's skeletons also lay thick on every side. Bones of the elephant principally; for among them lay huge tusks in quantities, tusks the like of which I had never seen, except in pictures of the giant mammoth of prehistoric ages, tusks the girth of a man in size. Piled in all directions they lay, the whole vast floor was indeed a stupendous charnel house. And among the white sand and bones diamonds lay thick as pebbles on a beach.

Across this floor ran the path now a raised causeway some feet above the level of the sand and about five hundred yards from where I stood the fire burnt in front of a building in the shape of a pyramid. Still no sign of life could I see and I made my way towards it. As I did so the sun's rays broke over the edge of the cliff above, and fell full upon the top of the pyramid, and another flame seemed to shoot from it, and remained there flashing brilliantly.

I was close to the fire now, and saw that it was no hand-fed flame, but a column that rose from an orifice in the rock, and burnt fiercely with a low roaring noise, and a strong mephitic odor. Probably it was some kind of natural gas; at any rate there was no one near it and nothing to fear from it. The pyramid behind it was made of ivory, thousands of tons of magnificent tusks going to make up its forty feet of height, and up it, in steps, ran the path, for the pyramid was the culmination of this road of dead. I climbed up and reached the apex, a platform some twenty feet square, above which something still towered, crowned by a flashing light.

Its brilliance dazzled me, and it was only by shading my eyes with my palm that I could discern what the object was that bore it.

Then, directly beneath the bright glare I gradually made out a gigantic face, glaring down upon me, a face carved with such wondrous art that, monstrous as it was, it appeared to live, and to be endowed with such awful malevolence that for a moment I shrank back in dismay. It was the face of a woman, but the body that it crowned was that of a snake, and was coiled round an ivory pillar rising from the platform. Marvelously fashioned of bronze, the face, with bared serpent fangs, bent down as though to strike: and set in a strangely fashioned diadem above the brows was a gigantic diamond, as large as a man's head, and of such blinding luster that it was impossible to look closely at it as well try to gaze full at the midday sun.

It was an idol, undoubtedly; a Moloch waiting for a sacrifice; and as my fascinated eyes at length left the face of terror, and passed down the coiled body and ivory pillar, I saw that the sacrifice was already there. For at the base lay a dead man, and his blood was scarcely dry upon the altar.

He was fast bound with hide thongs to stanchions cut in the rock a man almost as white as myself, with long, straight black hair, and clothed in clean white flowing robes. His face was horribly disfigured, seared and burnt as though by red-hot irons, and his features quite indistinguishable. Apparently, then, he had been tortured, before being stabbed to the heart by the strangely fashioned knife of bronze that lay beside him.

It is beyond me to describe the terror with which the sight of this dead and mutilated victim inspired me. I had seen no human being for so long: dead Inyati's face had been the last that I had gazed upon; then, after long I had seen the skeleton in the pool the road of skulls and now at last I gazed upon a human form again, it was again that of the dead.

All around me was death, death everywhere, and I felt that unless I escaped, and found human companionship soon, my mind would give way beneath these horrors.

And I must quit this place of sacrifice at once, for the fiends who had laid this victim there would probably give me but scant mercy were I found there.

I examined the body again: it might well have been that of a South European, so light was the skin; and now I noted that on one wrist was a copper bracelet exactly similar to the one Inyati had given me, and which I now wore on my own wrist. I compared them, and found them identical, and now I noted that the rude attempt at a snake's head into which their fastenings were fashioned, was undoubtedly an imitation of the head of the idol above me.

This, then, doubtless was Inyati's land, and this one of the priests he had spoken of. Mayhap he had killed one of them and taken his bracelet before he fled for he had spoken of jealousy and of a woman I---

But of the idol, the road, the craters he had said nothing . . . maybe he knew not himself?

True, he had feared the priests, till the "little gun" had become his with it he would, doubtless, have faced all the priests living but I, looking at the dead man and realizing something of the manner of his death, was in deadly fear . . . my revolver would be but little use against fiends who served their own priests thus!

I must fly from this place at once if indeed it were not already too late! But gaze as I could, no sign of life showed anywhere; no sound broke the silence except the low hissing murmur of the flame that burnt everlasting incense to the shrine of horror before me.

And so, glancing from side to side in mortal terror, starting at the sound of my own soft footsteps, and feeling that unseen eyes watched me from all sides, I left the Snake and its victim, the pyramid and the flame, and fled swiftly along the causeway, not even stooping to pick up the diamonds that lay on all sides, intent only upon escape. I reached the entrance, and passed through the narrow portals and breasted the steep slope, and fearful and over-wrought, I gained the open plain again.

Northward lay the path to the mountains: south the labyrinth of craters I had left; westward mayhap I should find the dunes? And pitiless as they were, I chose that path rather than follow the road of skulls towards the country and the mercy of such fiends as these people must be!

Soon I had left the crate far behind, and no trace of the road could be seen when I glanced back, but I could not shake off a haunting fear that now possessed me, that I was being watched. Eyes seemed to follow me everywhere, each bush or rock seemed to hide a watcher, and again and again I turned aside and searched, and looked fearfully over my shoulder, but nothing could I see.

And so I walked till evening, seeing no trace of the human beings I knew must be near, and at last, somewhat easier in mind, I threw myself down to sleep.

And awakened to find myself seized and held as in a vice, to feel thongs passed about me, and a hand passing over my forehead . . . gently . . . gently . . . and then all consciousness faded away.

VIII - THE CATACLYSM THE PRIESTESS "LOOK AND FORGET"

Now gazing down full upon me as though in exultation was again the awful face of the Snake, with its diadem the great, bright diamond. Its glare hurt me, and I tried to move my head, but in vain. I was tied fast.

And now I realized that this was no part of an awful dream, but that I lay a hopeless victim in the place of the tortured man I had seen but a day before.

And I knew that I was no longer alone, for though I could see nothing but the grim idol, I could hear around me the murmur of many tongues. Low, but vast in volume, it seemed as though thousands were there below me, hushed and waiting for the consummation of the sacrifice. At times the murmur rose to a mutter as of distant thunder, then again it would be hushed almost into dead silence.

I could not speak or move. I could only lie inert and helpless, filled with the agony of despair, with closed eyes awaiting the stroke, and praying silently that it would come before the mutilation I had seen on the other face.

Now came a single hoarse voice near me intoning words in a chant; and then in response broke out the deep roar of a multitude of voices! Higher and higher it rose until the air vibrated with its thunder, then again it would die away, fainter and fainter till it was nothing but as the sighing of wind through dead men's bones.

Again and again chant and response broke forth, and now too I could distinguish much of its meaning, for the tongue was that of Inyati.

A song of supplication it seemed to me, a song for the Snake's wrath to be appeased to accept the sacrifice offered it, and to send rain upon their dried up fields.

Now it died utterly away, and sweat broke from me in agony as I waited for I knew not what. I tried to make up my mind to die calmly, to resign myself to the inevitable; but my period of liberty and my new-found strength had brought back the old love of life that had burned strong in me before my captivity, and my whole being cried out passionately against this awful end.

Still there was silence, silence for a seeming eternity of waiting for the sharp sting of death . . . and then another voice lifted as though in invocation. Solemn, loud, clear and sonorous, the measured accents rang forth, from close beside me; a voice of unearthly beauty chanting a rhythmic sentence or two, repeated again and again. No hoarse voice of a man this, but of a woman . . . a priestess . . . calling down the fires of Baal to consume the sacrifice.

And, as if in response, came now the peal of heavy thunder.

I had been in terror of the knife before, but had lain silent and with closed eyes awaiting the end, but as the terrible significance of the song of invocation reached me, a hoarse cry of horror broke from my parched throat, and I again tried in vain to struggle free. For now my staring eyes confirmed the terrible thought that had come to me. The sun would soon be exactly overhead, and when it was, its rays would strike exactly through the huge diamond that crowned the Snake, and the intolerable rays, thus concentrated as though by a mighty burning glass, would fall full upon my eyes, torturing and searing me to the semblance of what I had seen on the dead priest.

Screaming and writhing in an agony of apprehension, I lay helpless, whilst the sun sped on, until its rim had almost reached the diamond. But now came peal after peal of terrific thunder, and vivid lightning that made even the sun look pale, and speeding across my field of vision came also a huge black cloud thick and ominous, but to me a most blessed sight a messenger of mercy a miracle! Swiftly it sped, but would it be in time?

The sun had reached the diamond now, and shrink as I would I already felt the roasting heat that beat upon the stone but a few inches from my head. Surely it would reach me, my brain would crack . . . but now, thank God! . . . the cloud had swept across, and for the moment I was safe, at least from this terror.

And now, with the almost incessant roar of thunder came the rain a few huge, stinging drops at first then a downpour such as I had never seen. In incessant sheets it fell like a huge cataract, beating upon my helpless face till I gasped for breath, as one half drowned; and soon the roar of water falling upon water almost drowned the pealing thunder. The shouts of joy that had hailed the first few drops were soon changed to wild cries of alarm, and as still the deluge continued as though the very flood-gates of heaven were opened, the screams of the vast multitude joined the roar of water and the pealing of thunder in one stupendous chorus. I could not see, but I could hear and realize that an awful struggle was going on below me: there in that vast hollow the unseen people would be trapped beyond hope, for into it the water from the plains above would rush in one vast cataract. And still the torrent beat down and the thunder pealed; and I, half mad with my sufferings, yelled and shouted, in mockery of the screams of those who would have immolated me, and who were now themselves perishing all around me. At length the groans and screams of the dying multitude died down to choking gasps, then even these ceased, but still the thunder pealed, and the rain beat down upon my unprotected body till my overwrought senses rebelled, and I sank into a swoon.

A voice the voice that I had heard in invocation came to me in my disordered dreams calling me back. Its insistence troubled me, for I was unwilling to return. But again and again it called, and I at length came back reluctantly to reality.

"Fear not, thy life is thine own again," said the grave, vibrant accents in my ear, and I opened my eyes to find myself still lying upon the altar.

Gazing down upon me was a face that I shall never forget to my dying day the face of a woman, whose skin of ivory whiteness accentuated the unfathomable blackness of the most wonderful eyes I shall ever behold.

They seemed to pierce me through and through, and to search my very soul, as I lay there and gazed back into them as a fascinated bird gazes back into the eyes of the striking snake.

Power infinite there was in those commanding orbs, wisdom and knowledge surpassing that of mere mankind infinite good or infinite evil I know not which!

I shrank in mortal terror at their merciless scrutiny, but I could neither close my eyes nor tear them away, until a hand was passed across my brow, and the spell was broken.

Now a knife cut my bonds, and I was raised by a strong arm to a sitting posture.

How is it possible to describe the horror of the appalling scene that met my shrinking eyes, as for the first time since I had been a prisoner I was able to look upon my surroundings.

The blood-red sun was setting in a stormy sky, from which in the distance the lightning still flickered, close beside me stood the tall form of the priestess, and below, on the lower tiers of the pyramid, were grouped about twenty men priests I judged them to be all robed in white garments, all white men, of fierce and sinister aspect.

But it was not upon these that my eyes rested, but upon the grim and awful holocaust that stretched in all directions below and beyond.

For the pyramid stood as an island in a sea of dead men: from its base, to the mighty walls that encircled the vast floor of the crater, it stretched in an unbroken sheet unbroken, that is, except for the myriad drowned bodies from which the rapidly receding flood was fast draining away.

The glare from the crimson sunset turned it into a sea of blood, and each moment the forms of the drowned multitude showed more and more distinctly; clasping and clinging to each other in the awful contortions of death, as they had struggled with each other in their frantic fight against that awful cataclysm; heap upon heap, line after line, thousands upon thousands of them a multitude a whole nation overwhelmed and destroyed.

Not white men such as the priests, who alone had been saved upon the pyramid, but brown men of Inyati's type, their bodies nude except for a loincloth.

Stunned and dismayed at the fearful sight, I sat inert upon the altar, and gazed upon the mighty hecatomb in utter forgetfulness of my own awful position, till the priestess, who had awakened me, and who also had stood in silent contemplation, turned and once more fixed her glowing eyes upon me.

"Look well, O stranger, look well upon these thy dead," she said in a clear, ringing voice; "upon these who would have sacrificed thee yet who, dying, called upon thee, their bound sacrifice, to save them! 'Save us, Mighty One!' they supplicated, 'thou who art mightier than the Snake save us!' . . . Poor fools they are dead all, all, are dead. . . . And thou, thou helpless 'Mighty One'" she mocked, "art thou content with this thy vengeance, or must we poor servants of the Snake also die to appease thy wrath?"

The look and tone of fierce mockery brought back to me all the fear of hideous torture I had felt before, and I begged that they should mercifully kill me and have done.

"Nay," she replied, "fear not that shall not be I have told thee thy life is safe. Well do I know that thou art but a man, and no god, such as these poor fools thought thee at the last but the Snake hath spared thee, and thy life is sacred. Free shalt thou go, free and with an abundance of the bright stones these dead people deemed sacred and the lust of which brought thee, O stranger, unasked and unwelcome to this our land. Life shall be thine and thou shalt be guided back to the land from whence thou earnest; but thou shalt eat first of the fruit of forgetfulness, and never shalt thou find again the path by which thou earnest hither, or that other by which thou shalt return."

The solemn tone and promise allayed my fears somewhat; at least my life was to be spared; but this talk of not finding the path again did it mean that they would blind me?

Even as the thought entered my mind the mysterious being who held me in her power answered it as though I had spoken it aloud.

"Fear not, I say again," said she, "neither thine eyes, nor a hair of thy head shall be injured. Rather do I grant thee a precious boon, such as many crave for in vain the boon of forgetfulness . . . yet not of all! Stand upon thy feet, O stranger, and look well upon this lake of the dead, then turn and look upon me these things thou shalt not forget."

Weak and shaken by my awful experience, I tottered as I tried to stand upright, and but for her supporting hand I should have fallen. "Aye thou art weak," said she again, "but that which I will give will bring back the strength to thy palsied limbs. . . . Look well, I say, and forget not this!"

Forget! How could I ever forget that awful scene the blood-red water, the countless heaps of drowned men, the upturned faces of the pale priests below me, their dark eyes fixed upon me with looks of hatred and malevolence.

"Aye, they would torture and sacrifice thee," said the strange being who dominated them, and who held my life in her hands, and who again answered my unspoken thought, "but that may not be. . . . And now look thou on me and forget not."

She stood proudly erect, her brow bound by a bronze snake the miniature of the idol above, the diamond set in this strange coronet outdone in splendor by the fires of her wondrous eyes. And now I saw her not as a sphinx-like being of terror, but as a glorious woman, a creature to be adored for her beauty alone, and the long stagnant blood coursed through my veins as I gazed entranced, and for ever enthralled.

No thought of that woman who waited crossed my mind, nothing but mad desire and adoration filled me for this creature of unearthly beauty;

and spirit, woman, devil, be she what she might, my one mad longing was to gaze upon her, to worship her, to possess her for ever.

And as I gazed spellbound she spoke again.

"Nay, I see thou wilt never forget," she smiled gravely, "yet must thou eat of the fruit that will bring forgetfulness of all other things."

She called to the priest in another tongue; and one came scowlingly, bringing with him a small box of ebony. The priestess took something from it, and again turned her piercing eyes upon my own, compelling, commanding, dominating me, as she had done when I first opened my eyes. I tried to speak to beg, to implore, that I might remain her slave, if need be, but near her, but she had put a spell upon my tongue, and I could not.

Slowly she held forth her hand, and in the palm I now saw a small withered berry, black and shriveled, but in shape like the scarlet berries I had eaten so often in the crater. "Eat and forget! . . . Eat and forget!" the voice commanded; and now the eyes sought mine again and fascinated and mastered me.

No! I would not eat. ... I would not go! and with all my strength I opposed her will . . . this was poison surely ... I would not eat!

"I seek not thy life rather would I save it," came the warning, as I struggled against the domination, "I have but to hold forth my hand to these my servants, and they would tear thee limb from limb. See, then!"

A gesture, and the crowd of frowning priests sprang up the steps and swarmed round me; their fierce, vulpine faces aglow with terrible joy, their long talon-like nails outstretched to rend me fearful horrifying!

At a word, and just as they had almost reached me, the priestess stayed them; but now their hot breath beat close upon me, and in deadly fear I stretched out my hand and took the berry. "Eat eat, and be safe, no harm shall come thee eat and forget eat and forget!" and with the clarion accents ringing in my ears, and with those unfathomable eyes gazing steadily into my own, I crushed the berry between my teeth and swallowed it. A strange, acrid taste, similar but vastly stronger than the berries I had eaten before . . . a rush of blood to my head, a tingling through all my veins, and then a blackness surging up and hiding all, even blotting out the star-like eyes before me, till all, all was black.

An endless dream of wanderings in thick pathless forests, an endless search for something lost: an eternity of vague formless dreams. Searching searching, and finding nothing: an infinite sorrow for something I could never again find.

Eyes gleaming at me from the dark forest; a myriad eyes, coming and going in the vague shadows, and a voice calling; something I could not

understand; and through all, the sorrow for something precious, lost
beyond recall.

IX - FORTY YEARS! THE AWAKENING

And then voices in my own tongue, low voices in the tongue I had not
heard for so long; and kind English faces coming and going beside my
bed, and mingling with my dreams.

And there came a time when I awoke to full sanity again, a time when
dreams no longer blended with reality.

I lay in a cool, green-shuttered room, and beside me sat a pleasant-
faced man, dressed in white, who was looking at me intently, and who
nodded vigorously as I looked back at him.

"Better, eh?" he asked "There, don't speak. I can see you are. Take
this, and go to sleep; you have had a bad time, and must get stronger
before you talk."

And strong I got rapidly, and in a few days he told me where I was,
and how I came there.

He was the British Consul at Loanda in Portuguese West Africa, and
one morning about two months before, some natives had brought me in
to him slung in a machilla.

They said they had been paid to bring me in, and that I was sick, and
before he had had time to question them closely they had disappeared,
without anyone finding out where they came from.

Sick and delirious, the Consul had been on the point of sending me
to the Portuguese hospital, when a few words in English caught his
attention, and feeling that he could not leave a fellow-countryman to the
mercy of strangers and foreigners in such a plight, he had seen me
through the stiff bout of brain fever in his own house.

As he told me all this, I decided to tell him all in return; for I now remembered all that had happened up to the time I had swallowed the
berry; though after that it seemed nothing but a dream.

And first I asked him if the natives had brought anything with me.
"Nothing whatever," he replied, "except a small skin bag of stones!"

He had not opened it, nor did I need to then, for the feel was enough.
And it had been no dream then the crater, the deluge, the priestess, and
the promise she gave me.

Quietly, and as briefly as I could, I told him my story. Half way
through it he stopped me. "Look here," he said, "you mustn't go on like
this. You are wandering again!" and though I assured him I was not, he

felt my pulse and took my temperature. Then he let me go on again, and though he looked puzzled and uneasy he listened till I was finished. And then, looking at his pained and startled expression, I could see that he believed I was lying or mad.

And then and then only I opened the bag. And the diamonds were there enough to make a dozen men rich many more than the few blue ones I had with me when I first escaped.

And never was a man more astounded than the Consul; again and again he made me repeat my story, and at last, in considerable agitation, he got up and walked to the window, where he stood looking out in silence for some time.

Then he came back to the bed where I lay, and looked searchingly at me again.

"You are a young man," he said slowly; "to all appearance you are a young, strong man in spite of your scarred face and your bent spine, you look a young man! Now how long were you there in that pit how long do you think has passed since your terrible experience with the Snake?"

"It all seems like a dream," I answered him, "and I cannot tell. But I must have been several months in the crater perhaps a year. Since then I cannot have wandered long."

"Well, then," he questioned, "what month and year was it that you went to Walfisch Bay, and found Inyati?"

"In 1860," I said; "I landed there in November, 1860. What is it now?"

"Good God, man," he exclaimed, "you must be mistaken. Are you sure it was 1860?"

"Sure," I repeated, "November, 1860; and it was some time in the following May that I lost Inyati May, 1861. Last year, was it?"

"Last year! Last year!" he repeated as though dazed in fact I could see that he was absolutely frightened. "Why man, what you tell me is incredible impossible! If it were true, you have slept for nearly forty years. For it is now 1900."

And now it was my turn to be amazed, for truly what he had told me was incredible . . . surely he must be mad himself!

But he went to the door and called the little Portuguese doctor, who had also been kindness itself to me.

"Aha," he said as he looked me over and felt my pulse, "now you are well and have sense again, eh? That is good, it is good that you are strong very strong never have I see so strong a man never! And if you have not been strong, you would die, for your head it was quite mad!"

"Look here, Doctor Santos," said the Consul, "our friend has forgotten a lot of what has happened to him, . . there is a long period about which his mind is a blank months in fact years!"

"That can be if it is the fever, yes! he will remember again. But his head have been hurt, it is to be seen, that too may make forget, for months even a year!"

"Forty years?" suggested the Consul tentatively.

"Ah, you joke, my friend!" replied Santos, "that would not be possible, he is surely not that age himself?"

And laughing, as he thought, at the Consul's joke, the little man gave me a few instructions that I did not even hear, and left us.

And the Consul, without a word, handed me a newspaper, and a glance at it was enough to show that he at least had made no mistake, for it was dated September, 1900.

And now I was like to go crazy again, with the shock and bewilderment. Forty years! A lifetime lost. My friends would be dead, or old, old people who had long forgotten me. Of what use would all this wealth be to me an old and forgotten friendless man. Old! yes, I must be an old, old man myself. And yet, now the fever had gone, I felt strong and vigorous indeed, the doctor had said that I was exceptionally strong and that I was not forty and the Consul too had said I was a "young, strong man!"

Surely this was pure hallucination . . . but no! the paper was real enough. And turning it over I saw that indeed I had slept a lifetime, for although it was in my own tongue, all it referred to was absolutely strange to me. New inventions, places I had never heard of, nations even that were unknown to me; it was as though I read of a new world, as, uncomprehending, I glanced through this first newspaper that I had seen for forty years.

The Consul had sat watching me in silence. He saw my agitation, and realized something of what I felt, for putting out his hand and grasping mine he said, kindly: "It must be a blow . . . friends all dead, eh? Well, I'm your friend, anyhow . . . and you'll remember later. Why, man, you must get that forty years out of your mind you are surely younger than myself, and will be as strong as a bull in a week or two. Try and sleep, my friend; you'll remember better to-morrow!"

But well I knew that the memory of those lost years would never return to me. "Eat and forget forget!" The words were ringing in my ears even now, as though spoken but yesterday. I had but to close my eyes and the scene of deluge and destruction, there beneath the Snake, came as a vivid picture before them and the eyes and voice of the woman that had bade me forget were with me always. Those burning eyes! They blotted out every other vision even that of the woman that had waited. God help me, I could not even remember the semblance of her face always those eyes of flame came between us. And God help her! If she had waited all these years she would be an old, old woman but forty years! Surely she was dead!

When had it been, that awful sleep of mine that had blotted out nearly half a century, and left me, an anachronism, an outcast a "young, strong man" still, whilst my schoolmates must be old, toothless gossips or long since dead and forgotten? It must have been in the crater where I had fallen that all these years had passed!

The strange berries, mayhap they had robbed me of these years the berries that stupefied me and gave me pleasant dreams.

What then had the priestess bidden me forget . . . the path? Yes, the path; and truly my wanderings had been but as a confused dream, a long weary search it had seemed, hopeless and endless, yet it could have taken but a few months from that long total of years.

And the thought came to me that though I knew nothing of this way of my return, yet the spell had not been perfect, for I forgot little of that other path I had trod with Inyati, and after; and I could, and would, return!

For as my strength came back, and grew till it was the wonder of all, so did my longing to return increase.

The eyes the voice that had bidden me go, now seemed to call for me incessantly . . . all else was a weariness I must go back!

For long I fought it. I even went back to England with Gerard, my good friend the Consul, who, if he still thought me mad, at least respected my madness.

For he said nothing of my story to a soul, and he it was that piloted me as a child through the new conditions of life that I found on all sides in England; he helped me turn part of my diamonds into a large fortune, he helped me at length and with reluctance, for he would rather not have believed in the miracle of my long sleep to find proof of all I had told him.

There came a day when we stood before the graves of my father and mother, who had died years after I had left England died mourning me as dead and from the lips of an old greybeard, who had been my schoolmate, we heard how that scapegrace son of theirs had gone treasure-seeking and had never returned all those years ago.

Poor old garrulous fool; he little knew that the deformed, but strong and vigorous man that asked him of this companion of his youth was that very "scapegrace" himself transformed, and with age held back from him by a miracle.

And there came a day, too, when a sweet-voiced, silver-haired old lady, with her grandchildren playing about her, told these two strangers from Africa how her lover of long ago had gone there to win her a fortune, and had never returned, and how she had waited ten long years for him, till all hope of him had fled, before she married; and how even now she held his memory in dear regard.

How astonished and delighted she had been at the blazing diamond I had given her, in memory of that old adventurer, of whom we said we had heard in far-off Africa; and how I feared as she looked in my eyes, that she would know. For as she gazed tearfully at me, and stammered her protests and thanks for she was poor, and it meant wealth to her I saw her eyes widen as they looked into my own, and she stammered: "You! . . . who are you? . . . You have his very eyes, are you his son?"

Almost was I tempted to tell her all, but the Consul's warning glance stayed me; and why, indeed, should I change her sweet memory of me as I had been, into the horror and dismay she must feel if she knew all?

And so I left her happy, and she blessed me as I went; blessed me as a mother might do for indeed I was apparently young enough to be her son and to her amongst all the women of my own land my disfigurements were as nothing, for she was of those wise and sweet beings that see deeper than the surface.

And then I came back, for I was as a lost man there in the rush and worry of a civilization I knew nothing of moreover, never could I rest, for the eyes of that other being were haunting me and calling me . . . calling me. . . . Well she had known spirit, woman, witch, or what she may have been that once I had looked in her eyes I might forget all else, but her I should forget never.

And so I have sought for years . . . and I cannot find the path.

Again and again I have tried from all sides. West, where Inyati led me, the dunes have altered; storm after storm has swept them till many of the pans are filled and covered, and others laid bare; and from the south it is the same.

Eastward I have tried in vain, for Khama's men are jealous guardians of the desert border there, and twice I have been turned back, in spite of my gold.

From the north and through it I must have found a path back I have struggled long, and there fever has killed my men, and pathless forests have kept me back.

There I left Gerard in a lonely grave; for after he knew that my story had been true nothing could keep him from joining me. Life in Loanda was far too tame, with such an adventure in hand. "Hang the diamonds," he had said, "I've money enough for my simple needs. But those berries they are what I want, for I am getting old, and would be young again. And this woman you dream and rave of perhaps I would see her too!"

Poor friend, he lies there in the thick forest where the fever took him he had not my strength.

And now I go again this time alone. I have searched these dunes till but one path remains untried on that path I now travel. And this time I shall not strive in vain, and again I shall look into those eyes that I have worshipped so long.

And then? Who knows? I am no trembling fugitive now, but one who fears not to measure strength with the immortals if needs be. ... If she be that, I fear nothing . . . and I shall find the way. Seek not to follow me, my friend of the wilderness . . . for I leave no spoor. . . . This time I shall find the path.

It was nearly morning when he finished his weird tale; the waning moon had risen, and threw a faint light over the limitless void of the desert.

The fire was dying down, and I turned to replenish it; for lions were numerous in the vicinity. And as I turned back, I saw this strange acquaintance of mine for the last time. He stood about twenty yards away, his arms outstretched towards the desert as though in supplication; a motionless and striking figure in spite of his deformity.

"I'm going to turn in," I called; but he neither moved nor answered, and when I looked again he had gone.

"He will be back directly," I thought, and curling myself up on my blanket I fell asleep immediately.

All too soon my boys called me, and waking, I found that my guest had gone.

"Which way?" I asked Jantje.

"Nie, baas; ek wiet nie," he said, shaking his head.

"Kambala," said I, impatiently, to the other man; "has the ou baas gone?"

"Ee-wah t In-koos," he answered in the affirmative; "but where I know not. Ask thou, master, these Bushmen, they know!"

There were two Bushmen in the camp, who had turned up but the day before and I made Kambala bring the small, pot-bellied men to where I sat. I knew their "talk."

"The baas with the scarred face," I said; "whither went he?"

"No! no!" they answered in their clicking tongue, "we know not! Who knows? Not we 'Khoi Khoian.'"

"Ye are no 'Khoi Khoian' (Hottentots, as Bushmen often like to style themselves), but San (Bushmen), and of these parts. Therefore, answer me where is he, that scarred one?"

They squatted on their haunches before me, looking at me furtively from their little slits of eyes, muttering to each other afraid.

"Master, we fear," they said reluctantly. "He is a great witch, that 'old one' we know him well. Often does he cross the dunes where even we dare not go where no man goes!"

"Seek him," I ordered.

"No! no!" they said again, "he leaves no spoor and we fear. It is not well to follow that 'old one'!"

And search as I could, no spoor did I find.

But what I did find, there on my blanket beside my pillow, was a big, blue, uncut diamond, together with a scrap of paper bearing the one word "Farewell."

2.   THE SALTING OF THE GREAT NORTH-EASTERN FIELDS

THE SALTING OF THE GREAT NORTH-EASTERN FIELDS, BEING AN EPISODE IN THE LIFE OF DICK SYDNEY, PROSPECTOR

CHAPTER I

To be "broke to the world" was by no means a new experience to Dick Sydney, and as he sat on the sandy shore near Luderitzbucht and watched the setting sun turn the broad ocean into molten gold, he was little troubled by the fact that his last mark had been spent an hour or two back for a very belated and necessary breakfast, and that he was now absolutely penniless. Always an optimist, Dick easily outdid the immortal Micawber in his faith in something turning up just when things looked their blackest, and he had literally no thought for the morrow, until his hand, mechanically groping in his pocket for the wherewithal to fill his pipe, advised him of the fact that even his "baccy" was finished.

This was serious, for Dick's old battered briar rarely left his mouth; and whilst the odoriferous Boer equivalent for the "divine weed" held out, food and drink were but minor considerations. But something must be done now, so, knocking out the ashes from his last whiff, and with one more futile grope in his capacious pocket, he stuck his empty pipe in his mouth, rose, stretched himself, and, glancing once more at the pageant of the western sky, turned back towards the contemptible collection of tin shanties, drinking saloons, empty beer-bottles, and Germans, known as Luderitzbucht.

A few months back, the discovery of diamonds had brought fame to this wind-swept wilderness, and fame had been immediately followed by the choicest collection of cosmopolitan scoundreldom that a mining "rush" had ever been responsible for.

Now Dick Sydney, though a man of variegated experience and a bit of a "hard case," was still passing honest, and a gentleman; and he soon found that he stood but little chance in Luderitzbucht. His modest capital, which he had hoped to increase in this new Diamondopolis, had vanished within a few weeks of his arrival, swallowed up by shares in diamond-fields that existed only in the vivid imagination of the swindling "company-promoters" or so-called "prospectors," who infested the place; and when his illusions of easily-made wealth had vanished also, and he had tried to obtain a billet, he had failed utterly.

His knock-about experiences had included several spells of gold-prospecting and mining in California and other wild spots, and, being as hard as nails, he was admirably suited to the life of a prospector, and prospectors were being paid large salaries in those early days of the diamond rush in German South-West Africa. But, unfortunately for himself, Dick possessed a constitutional but at times embarrassing prejudice against lying, and in his numerous applications about prospecting jobs had made no secret of the fact that his prospecting had never been for diamonds.

And as a result he had had to stand aside and see all sorts of gentry taken on for the numerous expeditions that were constantly being arranged: runaway seamen, cooks, stewards, and stokers from the ships, gangers and navvies from the railways, ne'er-do-wells of all descriptions, with but here and there an old "river digger," or genuine prospector to leaven the lump.

Added to his stubborn and uncompromising honesty, Dick possessed another trait which severely handicapped him in this German-governed dust-hole of creation, in that he was uncompromisingly British, and took no pains to conceal the fact; and here in Luderitzbucht the arrogance of the German officials, and the way in which they boasted of Their Army, and Their Kaiser, and Their Beer, and Their Sauerkraut, and, in short, of every product of their whole blamed Fatherland, exasperated Dick to a degree. Though not very big, he was a bundle of muscle and sinew, and already he had been fined heavily for making a mess of one or two spread-eagled Teutons who had been unwise enough to mistake his quiet manner for timidity.

Dick strolled back over the low-lying sand-dunes to the little town-ship, where lights were already twinkling in the stores and beer- halls; and, passing the largest of these, he suddenly realized that he was thirsty, and, momentarily forgetting the state of his finance, he turned into the bar for a bottle of beer. The brightly-lit room was full of people, naturally mostly Germans, who, whilst imbibing vast quantities of their national beverage, were singing, bragging and swearing at the top of their voices, and after the manner of their kind. At the farther end of the room a big corpulent swashbuckler was holding forth loudly to a circle of admiring cronies; his peroration was an introduction to a toast; that toast was "To the Day!"

Dick had heard it frequently of late; in fact, wherever Germans and beer came together, that toast was being drank at the time.

"The Day!" . . . Dick, and every other Britisher knew what "Day" was meant, and as a rule took but little notice of these fire-eating gas- bags; anyway, though he understood German, he spoke it but little. And so he stood quietly imbibing his bottle of beer whilst Bombastus Furiosis still held forth. His quiet attitude evidently misled the orator, whose guttural German became mixed with quite enough English to make his remarks perfectly understandable to the few Britishers amongst the crowd.

Boasting and bragging, and with his discourse liberally garnished with "Donner-wetters," and such-like meteorological expressions dear to the Teuton, this big chap let the world at large know what would happen on the great "Day"; when the whole "schwein-hund" Englander nation would, at long last, be knocked sky-high and to everlasting flinders by the ineffable and invincible Army of Kaiser Wilhelm II.

Dick got tired of the drunken man's blatant boasting, and finished his beer with the intention of leaving the bar before he lost his temper, but as he put down the empty mug he realized with consternation that he had not the wherewithal to pay for the drink! He stood embarrassed and irresolute. What could he say to excuse himself how explain before this crowd of contemptuous Germans?

At that moment, however, something happened to put the matter out of his mind entirely. The orator had gone one better, and was now describing what various kinds of "schwein-hunden" all Britishers were, and those in Luderitzbucht in particular, when suddenly a small man, who had been sitting quietly in a corner of the room, left his seat, and, walking up to the group, called out, "'Ere, you with the mouth! Shut yer fat head abaht Englishmen or I'll make yer! I'm English. Wot yer got to say abaht it?"

A roar of laughter went up from the Germans, any of whom looked big enough to eat the small man. Dick pushed nearer to the group. He knew the chap now--he was a little Cockney Jew, a bookmaker, horse-dealer, and what not, scarcely the kind of chap to be expected to show pluck and patriotism, yet these are often met with in the most unexpected places. There he stood, opposite a German big enough to eat him and in fluent Cockney he proceeded to tell that big man more about himself than is good for any fat man to know.

Of course it could not last long. The jeering laughter changed to threats and curses, and then suddenly the colossus made a terrific round-arm all-embracing swipe at that small man, calculated to obliterate him once for all. But he wasn't there when it arrived; and, to Dick's joy and amazement, he saw the little Jew dodge in under the stroke, and with a spring and a lightning blow on the point bring down the big bully with a crash to the floor.

"A boxer, by gad!" yelled Dick, capering with excitement; "bravo, little 'un!" But the small man's victory was only that of a moment. The next the whole crowd had flung themselves upon him, and the miniature champion of "Rule Britannia" was borne to the ground in the centre of a whirl of legs, arms, chairs, bottles, and the other weapons usually preferred by the German larrikin to bare fists.

Dick could stand no more, and the members of that Peace Conference must have thought about that time that a cyclone had struck them.

It was no time for fancy boxing. Two men who faced Dick went down like ninepins before a terrific left and right between wind and water; a big Bavarian hero brandishing a beer-bottle collapsed with a sudden and acute attack of knee-in-the-stomach; and a strong and handy chair coming to Dick's hand in the nick of time and used as a flail, and with strict impartiality, soon did the rest. Berserk with fight, and with the plucky little Jew to help him, Dick cleared the bar till not a soul but the frightened bar-keeper and themselves stood within the locked doors. Outside they could hear the crowd yelling for the police.

"Mein Gott, mein lieber Gott! Who will pay for all der smashes?" whimpered the bar-keeper, wringing his hands, and looking round at the trail of the cyclone.

"Tell the truth abaht that big fat 'ed starting the row to the police, and I'll pay for the smash," said the little Jew. "And while we're waiting for the police let's have a drink," he continued. "Here's your health, guv'nor; blimey, but you're a bit useful in a scrap!" By this time the police were pounding at the door. "My money my money!" again pleaded the bar-keeper.

"Right-oh!" said the Jew, putting his hand in his pocket. His face changed; quickly and anxiously he searched for his pocket-book it was gone! Whilst they had had him on the floor they had improved the occasion; and his blank stare of dismay was mirrored on Dick's face as the latter remembered that he too was penniless and owed for a drink!

"Schwein-hunden! Thieves! Robbers! Dam-fools!" yelled the exasperated bar-keeper, unlocking the door for the police. That night they slept in a German prison.

CHAPTER II

Sydney could not disguise from himself the fact that the situation was rather serious. The escapade would probably mean a sentence of a stiff bout of imprisonment, or a heavy fine, and, as he was penniless, it would perforce have to be the former.

"Hang that little Yiddisher!" he growled, as he sucked at his empty pipe; "wish I'd let him get out of his trouble himself. No! I couldn't have done that. He's a plucky little beggar, and I suppose he's as bad off as myself now his pocket-book's gone. Still, I suppose something'll turn up."

His optimism was justified, for about ten o'clock the following morning he was liberated without more ado, and outside the gaol he found the little Hebrew who had been the cause of all the trouble.

"I squared 'em," explained the little man, with a grin; "sent a note along to a pal of mine who knows the ropes, and he soon got us out. Better come along and have some grub!"

"Look here," said Dick, "I'd better let you know right away that I'm dead-broke."

"Never mind," said the other; "come along and feed, and then we'll yap."

A good meal, and a good smoke after it, and the little Jew said abruptly, "Now then, Mr. Sydney, I've found out a bit about you this morning, and if you want a job, I think I can get one for you. We want a straight man for something that's on, and I think you'll do."

"I'm game," said Dick, "if it's a straight deal."

"Straight as a die," replied Solstein or "Solly," as he liked to be called. "Let's get along the beach, we can talk there!"

Pacing along the sands, with no one to hear them but the sea-gulls, and with his old briar again charged with some real God-fearing cake tobacco, Sydney heard what it was that was required of him; and there and then Solly's offer was accepted.

Two days later an expedition, outfitted regardless of expense in Johannesburg, left Luderitzbucht to carry out a systematic testing of certain distant diamond-fields recently discovered and acquired by a local syndicate, and reported to be fabulously rich, so rich that an extremely large company talked of acquiring them in turn, and those in the know hinted at a huge flotation.

Money was therefore no object, and the party was both large and well- equipped. It consisted of a diamond expert acting on behalf of the Syndicate; another expert acting on behalf of the would-be purchasers, and, incidentally, to watch the other chap; a financial representative of either side to watch proceedings; two prospectors, presumably to watch each other; a learned professor of geology to give an unbiased report of the fields; and, lastly, Dick Sydney, ostensibly in charge of the transport, but in reality to watch the whole caboodle of them.

Striking north-east, the expedition almost immediately entered a practically untraversed desert of barren sand-dunes, waterless, and both difficult and dangerous to traverse; and their animals drank nothing for the first two days. On the third, however, guided by the discovering syndicate's prospector Grosman, and by two stunted little Bushmen in his employ, they came to a deep water-hole, where the precious fluid, though "brak" (alkaline) and stagnant, was still plentiful and drinkable, and within working distance of which the newly-discovered "fields" were located. Here the dunes were interspersed with long narrow "aars," covered with fine gravel and loose stones, and here and there covered with scrubby vegetation.

Within a few days Sydney had to acknowledge that his first conclusion that there was not a single honest man in the party besides himself, was an unjust one, for the harmless and most necessary professor of geology was a notable exception.

Absorbed in his science, he passed most of his time in his tent poring over a microscope, taking very little heed, apparently, of what was going on, and he was obviously without guile and likely to be easily gulled by even the most transparent roguery. And that the others were rogues Dick grew more and more convinced, and it would have been hard to say which of the party he detested the more; Gilderman, the suave Johannesburg expert, glib, well-dressed and fastidious; Jelder, the syndicate's expert from the same locality, a rough-voiced, domineering mining engineer; Zweiter and Spattboom, the "financial" men; or Junes and Grosman, the two prospectors. On the whole, he thought, were he a free agent, he would have picked a quarrel with each and all of them for the sake of giving them individually a thrashing, and in that case the immaculate Gilderman would have been his first choice.

Each and all of them spoke English, and professed that nationality, but Dick soon decided that, with the possible exception of Junes, what wasn't German of the party was certainly Jew!

But still to all appearance everything was fair and above-board. The prospectors would point out the most likely spots to try for diamonds, the Ovampo boys would be set to work, and almost invariably they found diamonds. Occasionally one or other of the "experts" would suggest a different spot, and usually these sapient individuals would justify their reputation by finding diamonds also in these spots.

The syndicate's expert was jubilant, the company's expert apparently well satisfied, and the professor beamed upon the stones as they came from the sieve, talked learnedly of their origin and the peculiarities of the deposit they were found in, and passed a great deal of time in abstruse calculations as to the probable yield of the fields, based upon the rich finds they were making, and the genuineness of which he, obviously, never doubted.

Sydney picked up several small stones himself. The experts were always finding them, so were the financial agents; yet Dick, though for a time he could find out nothing to confirm his opinion, was convinced that the whole thing meant a gigantic swindle. A few words in French between the experts which they did not expect the "man in charge of the transport" to understand a word here, and a look there, strengthened this conviction into certainty, but still he had no proof.

Now Dick had heard of, and suffered from, more than one case of "salting" since he first came to Luderitzbucht, and the quantity of illicit diamonds in the hands of unscrupulous people made such salting a comparatively easy matter, but if it were being done in this case, it was certainly being done very thoroughly and artistically and when?

The whole party moved from place to place practically together in fact, they kept in sight of each other ostentatiously.

It must be done after dark, if at all, and Dick resolved to watch at night, as soon as he came to that conclusion. That same night, from his tiny patrol tent, he watched the lights go out one by one, until the camp lay silent, and apparently every one was asleep. And as time passed he was nodding himself, when suddenly a shadow stole silently from the tent occupied by the two prospectors, crossed to the experts' tent, and disappeared inside. Dick saw the momentary gleam of an electric torch and heard the tinkle of a bunch of keys, then the form reappeared, and, with a glance round, passed silently and rapidly out of sight across the sand-dunes.

Dick followed, the pale light from a waning moon, occasionally peeping from behind the clouds, making the pursuit an easy one.

After half an hour of rapid walking the man disappeared over a gigantic dune that Dick had noticed in the distance the previous evening, and which he had heard marked the position of the next field to be examined.

More cautiously now, and keeping well away from the man's actual spoor, Dick crept up the slope, and peered over the crest down the farther side.

The moon at that moment shone out clearly, and there, not fifty yards away from him, Dick could see the figure of Grosman the prospector. He was walking slowly up and down, now and then throwing his arm out with the action of a sower, and the seeds he sowed sparkled like dewdrops in the moonlight.

For he was sowing diamonds--salting!

CHAPTER III

Salting! there was no doubt about it.

The prospector to whom the syndicate owning the fields had entrusted the important task of locating the most likely spots on which to demonstrate their richness, had with admirable forethought forestalled that notoriously fickle jade Fortune and brought the diamonds along himself, before the remainder of the "testing" party arrived. To-morrow the whole caboodle of unbiased individuals, representing both his own party and the enormously wealthy Jo'burg financiers who were negotiating for the fields with a view to a big flotation, would come along as per schedule, and would doubtless be greatly impressed by this fresh proof of the fields' richness!

Dick lay flat on his face on the warm and accommodating sand-dune, and watched Grosman for some time: he was prodigal with the diamonds, and this was undoubtedly destined to be an exceptionally rich field.

"The question is," reasoned Dick, "how many of these swabs are in this swindle. Let's see now, it's no good letting my angry passions run away with me, and jumping on this chap as I'd like to do. I must reason this out. The other prospector sleeps in the same tent sometimes disagrees with this chap as to the best place to test. In that case yes! they've always tried and found in both places. And they sleep in the same tent. They're both in it. Same with the experts, both in the same tent, and they keep the diamonds. That's what this swab went to them to-night for. And Zweiter and Spattboom, well, no one could be honest with faces like theirs. Blazes! They're all in it, and all this elaborate business is just

to artistically fool the old professor--he's not part of the swindle, anyway."

That was it undoubtedly. The old professor, who, simple as a child in
many things, had yet a name famous the world over; he it was that this
precious crowd of scoundrels were deceiving so elaborately he it was
whose word of the genuineness of the finds would carry weight with the
financiers and when the time became ripe would rope in the guileless
public.

Well, he, Dick, would have to take a hand in it, but it would require
caution; moreover, Solly to whom he owed his job had told him at
parting:

"We don't want no experience, just you watch all of these blighters
and find out what their game is, and lie low that's all!"

His diamond sowing finished, Grosman sat down, took off his veldtschoens and knocked out the sand, loaded up his pipe, and with a sigh
of contentment which the pipeless and tobacco-loving Dick heard and
appreciated, turned back towards the camp.

Luckily Dick old hand on the plains of countries where it is not considered healthy to be found on the home trail of a man one watches at
night had taken the precaution to crawl aside sufficiently to give this
"Knave of diamonds" a wide berth; and he lay inert and silent as the
dead till Grosman was well on his homeward journey, before following
him to a well-earned spell of sleep.

Following the usual routine, the next morning the two prospectors
rode ahead to locate the best spot for proving this fresh field, the rest of
the expedition following more leisurely. Dick had to confess that they
were most artistic in their methods. On arriving near the high dune,
where he had seen Grosman giving Fortune a friendly lead in the small
hours of the morning, Dick found to his astonishment that they were
being guided to quite a different spot at some distance from the carefully
prepared "jeweller's shop." "What the devil does this mean?" mused he,
as he rode behind with the professor and the others. He could not be
mistaken about the spot, for the dune was too prominent a landmark yet
there were the two prospectors signaling to them from a place at least
half a mile away from the scene of his nocturnal experience. Trotting
across to them they found an argument in full swing.

"Gentlemen," said the other prospector a tall slab-sided individual
whose English was of a pronounced American flavor. "I don't think this
kind of thing is fair! I'm here earning the company's dollars, and I'm
about tired of being yanked around to try spots that Grosman points out.
I guess I'm here to locate the pay-dirt as well as he is, that's what the

company pays me for, that's what I'm here for, to find out the truth! No, sir not any I don't."

"Junes," cried Gilderman, "remember your position! I'm sure no one ever expressed a doubt as to the syndicate's finds and I--"

"But look-ee here, Mr. Gilderman," interrupted the prospector; "you've got to excuse me. I'm supposed to look into this thing myself, besides it's for the blamed fool's own benefit. Any fool can see that the deepest wash runs the other side of that dune, not this."

"Rot," jerked out Grosman; "well, if you want to go to your damned old place, do so."

High words followed, the experts became partisans, every one was dragged in except Dick and the Herr Professor, and the latter, flushed and rattled and his glasses all awry, was at length appealed to in the matter.

"Ach, gentlemens," said he, beaming from one to the other, and absolutely exuding good temper and conciliation; "why quarrel on this so-splendid an expedition, hein? Let us then return to the Herr Prospector Junes' choice let us accede to this so good man's request, hein?"

"Right," snorted Grosman; "but if the damned place is no good don't blame me and don't condemn the field. I can show you where there are stones, anyway!"

And so with many a sneer and jeer, and with an atmosphere of extreme tension pervading the whole party, Junes was allowed to lead the way to the spot of his choice. He went straight across the foot of the big dune, and in a few minutes had amply justified himself, for there were diamonds in abundance the diamonds his confederate Grosman had strewn there the night before.

Now Solly's instructions to Dick to lie low, and say nothing, no matter what he found out, had been explicit and insisted upon, and in spite of his instinct to warn the professor, he might have been content to "lie low" and go on watching till the trip was over, had it not been for a certain small but excessively highly-charged black scorpion that found its way into Dick's sleeping-bag that night; and more than making up in "cussedness" what it lacked in size, gave him an exceedingly warm time of it. One sting in particular, on a big vein in his leg, gave him excruciating pain, and though he applied the universal veldt remedy of nicotine from his pipe-bowl, the agony was so great and the swelling so alarming that at length he hobbled off to the professor's tent to see if that learned man could give him some relief. He found the old gentleman sleeping soundly and had some difficulty in rousing him; but that task accomplished, so assiduous was the professor in dressing the sting, and such kindly interest did he display in both Dick and the defunct scorpion, that Dick, who had always liked the old chap, almost made up his mind to tell him all that he had seen and suspected. The scorpion really settled the question for him, for the professor had scarcely finished injecting Dick's leg than he turned his attention to the dead reptile, at which he had already cast many curious glances as it lay on his little camp-table beside his medicine chest. And now he proceeded to examine it thoroughly, lighting a powerful acetylene lamp for the purpose.

And scarcely had the strong rays fallen upon the black, wicked, lobster-like little iniquity than the Herr Professor let off a regular yell of delight and literally fell upon Dick's neck.

"Ach, meine lieber!" he exclaimed ecstatically. "Aber this is most wunderbahr! It is of the great fortune, good luck, what you call him? That he sting you."

"Good luck?" said the surprised Sydney, feeling anything but pleased; "well, professor, it's the kind of luck that I can very well do without. Why, the blamed little thing must have been about a thousand volts strong. Sting! why it must have squirted about a pint of forked lightning into me! Luck?"

"Of the greatest," said the scientist; "of the most colossal. For it is a discovery you have of him made he is new he is wonderful wunderschoen wunderbahr!"

"You're wrong, professor," protested Dick with emphasis. "He discovered me. He may be new newly charged, anyway!"

"Of a variety entirely new, Herr Sydney," insisted the old professor impressively; "and much would I have given to have been in your place to discover him."

"You'd have been welcome," said Dick feelingly; "but why?"

"It is my life-work, my stedenpferd, my 'hobby' you call it, hein? This study of the arachnids, spiders, scorpions! Geology, you say? True, that is my work, but this other is different, this I love! Already have I four large volumes written upon the known varieties of scorpion and now to have been but almost the discoverer of a new variety, it is hard to have been so near. But at least I shall be the first to describe, to classify, that honor you will grant me? It is hard to have been so near!"

"Believe me, professor, it was a good deal harder to be just where I was. But I see your point, and feel for you indeed I may say I'm feeling it quite a lot even now. I'm mighty sorry the electric gentleman with the red-hot trousers didn't sample you first as you say, it's real hard he didn't. So do please take the fame and describe all you want!"

It took a lot of persuasion to make the scientist see it in the light that Dick did, but after a while he consented to name the new specimen after himself, and sat down to examine and gloat over his treasure.

But first he showed Dick some of his books, thick tomes full of illustrations of most weird and undesirable-looking insects, spiders, scorpions, and the like, and crammed with learned descriptions bristling with Latin names; and he showed such an innocent delight in his new acquisition that Dick's mind was made up. He did not like Germans, but this old chap was so naive, so full of human-kindness, so innocent and ignorant of all but his science that it would have been infamous not to have warned him of what was happening. For Dick could see plainly enough that if nothing were said this poor kind-hearted old scientist would have to bear the blame when the gigantic swindle was at length discovered, and the victimized public demanded a scapegoat.

He lifted the fly of the tent and looked out. There was no light in any of the tents, and the sound of snoring came from them in chorus. Farther away by the still flickering embers of the campfire could be dimly seen a dozen or more recumbent forms, where the native boys huddled. The waning moon was just rising, and except for the snores all was quiet as only the desert can be; yet Dick, when he turned once more towards the professor, stood with a warning finger on his lips, and spoke but in a whisper. For he knew that he and the man he spoke to were the only honest men in this lonely camp; and that the others would not hesitate to put either himself or the professor out of the way if once they suspected that their villainy was known, he never doubted. Not that he was afraid; but here in the wilds, with six well-armed and determined men against him, he saw the need for caution. The professor he did not count not just then!

The old man still sat at his little camp-table, magnifying glass in hand, and at Dick's low "Hist," he turned a bland, inquiring gaze in his direction. Dick came close to him, and with head half averted so that he could listen for the slightest sound outside, he whispered his story. Not a sound came either from the camp or from his listener till his brief tale was ended.

"They are all in it all rogues together, sir," he whispered in conclusion; "and it's part of a big swindle that people will blame you for."

And for the first time since he began his tale he looked the professor full in the face. He started with amazement as he did so: for now he saw not a benign, smiling old scientist, beaming good nature and affability through his spectacles, but a stern-faced, iron-mouthed man, whose jaw was set with grim inflexibility, and whose eyes seemed actually to blaze with fury. The big veins stood out upon his temples, and the hand that still held the magnifying glass was now clenched in a grip of iron, that trembled, not from weakness, but from the violence of his anger and emotion.

Dick saw the man with new eyes: this was no worn-out old scientist, such as he had deemed him; but a man still strong and vigorous, in spite of his three-score and ten years, a man in whom the hot blood of passion could still work wonders. And the younger man realized that if the strong hand were necessary in this affair, he would by no means need to play it alone.

"Gott im Himmel!" he muttered hoarsely, as Dick finished. "Diebstahl und rauberei! . . . and through me! For I have been a fool, and I have been also to blame. Look you, Herr Sydney, now can I see but too clearly that I have neglected my work, and looked but little to the fields themselves but to the diamonds and the gravel they brought with them. Numskull! dummkopf! That I have been it is but now that I see also how they have advantage taken of this hobby of mine. Each day they have brought me spiders, and scorpions, and snakes to examine even now I have almost a hundred specimens alive! And so they have thrown sand in my eyes, and would have made a criminal of me even as they are themselves. Schaendlich und verraetherisch schwein-hunden! But for you, friend, they would have robbed me of my good name, and shamed me before the world. But for you, friend!"

As he spoke, still in a hoarse whisper, he rose and grasped Dick's hand, and strong as the latter was he winced at the vigor of that iron grip.

"And now come!" said he, simply, turning as though to leave the tent.

Dick caught his arm. "No! no!" said he in a tense and eager whisper "what would you do?"

"Take them bind them disarm them . . . take them prisoners to Luderitzbucht to pay for their knavery," muttered the old man savagely. "Six and with arms, you say! And what care I for six such schwein- hunden? And you, Herr Sydney, I know you are both strong and fearless?"

"Oh, nothing would suit me better than to smash up the whole outfit, but what good would it do?" urged Dick. "It's their six words against ours, or rather against mine, so far! And most of 'em are German, as you know, and well in with the authorities in Luderitzbucht. And I'm English, what hope will my word have against theirs there? Besides, sir, the story as it stands will be all against yourself!"

"Donner-wetter, that is wahr! That will never do," said the old man naively. "What do you advise then?"

"Watch well, and either contrive to catch them yourself on some of the remaining fields or say nothing till we are safely back in Luderitzbucht," counseled Dick.

"Never can I so long contain myself with these thieves. Think you the company spoke of a flotation of 500,000, of half a million pounds, that these hounds would have caused my name and my report to rob from the public! Never can I contain myself long, but as you wish, friend, I will try unless indeed some better plan offers."

Dick crept back quietly to his little patrol tent and tried to sleep, but pain and excitement kept him wide-eyed; and he had scarcely dropped off when his Hottentot driver awakened him to tell him that two of the mules had broken their reins and cleared in the night, apparently making their way back in a bee-line towards Luderitzbucht.

"I have found their spoor, baas," he said; "but they have gone far and fast and it will need a horse to catch them."

"Saddle mine, quickly, and I will go back myself," ordered Dick, with a muttered blessing or two on the defaulters; and within a few minutes he was cantering over the spoor of yesterday, along which the mules had bolted. He soon found where they had left the trail, and in the now clear light of dawn their spoors showed clearly in the soft sand. At last he caught sight of them grazing on a small patch of Bushman grass growing in the hollow between two dunes, and after a considerable amount of trouble managed to secure them, and making them fast to a convenient bush he climbed a big dune to have a look round and try and mark out for himself a straight cut back to camp.

He recognized his whereabouts instantly, for scarcely five hundred yards away rose the big dune that had been the scene of Grosman's forethought two nights back. The sight of it brought back Dick's indignation afresh.

"Beastly swabs," he thought, "why they never even take the trouble to find out if there really are any diamonds in the blessed fields or not? From what I've seen at Kolman's Kop, this place looks extremely likely. I wonder whether, after all, they have been a bit too clever? I'll have a look, anyway."

Between him and the dune where the bogus find had been made there stretched a wide, flat space of comparatively firm ground a so-called anp, or shallow vlei, in which at some time water had accumulated. Here there was very little sand, its place being taken by a deposit of fine loose grit, made up of a variety of tiny stones all about the size of a small pea.

The prevailing wind, blowing almost continually in the same direction, had heaped up this grit in little wave-like ridges and Dick knew that if there were diamonds there he would find them near the crest of these little waves.

He went down on his hands and knees at once, and almost immediately his eye caught the glitter of a diamond. And there was another and another! And Dick, as he picked up stone after stone, realized that by sheer luck he had stumbled upon far the richest deposit he had ever seen or heard of and realized too that these clever scoundrels had over-reached themselves. There had been no need of salting had they but taken the trouble to search systematically they must have found this spot, had they but walked a few hundred yards from the spot they had salted last, this "Tom Tiddler's Ground" had awaited them!

Incredibly and incalculably rich it was; for Dick, in the hour or so that he permitted himself the luxury of picking them up, well-nigh filled his pockets with the glittering little gems, and yet he had scarcely moved a yard from where he had picked up the first.

The power of the blazing sun, now beating down upon him from high in the heavens, first admonished him of the fact that it was getting late, and that he must get back to camp, or probably some one would be coming to look for him.

"And that would never do," said Dick to himself; "no one must know of this but the professor."

So, reluctantly leaving his newly-found bonanza, he tied up the double- handful of diamonds in his old red handkerchief, thrust it in the bosom of his khaki shirt, and securing the two errant mules he struck across country to the camp.

He found that during his absence a farther field had been successful-ly "tested"; and the meaning look the professor gave him when the latter rode into camp with the returning party, and voiced his satisfaction at the morning's "find," left no doubt in Dick's mind but that the old man had profited by his advice, and would yet fool the would-be foolers! Itching as he was to impart the news of his splendid discovery to the professor, he had no opportunity of seeing him alone during the rest of the day; and he could only try to possess his soul with patience till night fell and the others were asleep. But that night the professor had a different plan in view.

"Gentlemens," said the old man when supper was finished, and they sat smoking by the fire; "now that this so successful expedition arrives at so near its conclusion, shall we not celebrate our good fortune? To-day is not our find of diamonds more rich than of ever? Let us drink then to our great good fortune, to the diamonds we have found, and to those we hope again to find to-morrow! Come!" He led the way to his tent, and diving under his bed he hauled out a case of wine. Strong, heady wine Dick found it, and the warning glance the old man gave him as he filled his glass the second time, made him sip but lightly of the potent liquor.

Not so the two experts, or the prospectors, or the other members of the little coterie of scoundrels; who, safe in the assumption that they had hoodwinked the professor thoroughly, drank deep and made merry like men without a care. Bottle after bottle was opened, and soon one of the experts began to snore; and it was the professor himself who broke up the merry party by saying: "Gentlemens; to-morrow have we a long day and a long ride before us to test the other fields. And the Herr Prospector Junes he must ride before us always, is it not? The test places to locate together with his comrade. And this so good man see! He sleeps already! Let us then to rest. But first fill again your glasses and drink deep. To the diamonds we have found and to the discovery you will make to-morrow!"

Surely the wine was very potent, for Dick, thanks to the warning glances of the professor, had drank but little, yet he could scarcely keep awake; whilst Junes and Grosman were snoring like pigs, and could scarcely be awakened sufficiently to enable them to stagger to their tent. Dick barely managed to get to his own before sleep overcame him too, and his last hazy thought was: "That wine was drugged, the professor must have got another plan!"

Once, in the night, he had a dim notion that some one was trying to waken him; that some one was it the professor? was shaking him and whispering fiercely in his ear, "Wake, man you must help me wake!" But it all seemed like part of a dream, and he was too overpoweringly sleepy to be able to rouse and the remembrance of this only came long after.

But at last he did awake; his head was buzzing and Andreas the Hottentot was shaking him. "Baas, baas; wake up," he was saying; "I cannot wake the others! Allemachtag! How they sleep like dead men!"

It was broad daylight; long past the hour when the prospectors should have ridden on ahead to locate the fields. Their horses, ready saddled, stood before their tent; and from it came the sound of stertorous snoring.

Dick walked over and shook the men; and at last they stumbled shakily to their feet, and made their way to the experts' tent, muttering something about instructions; but really, as Dick realized, to get the wherewithal to salt the remaining claims.

Usually this proceeding was carried out long before daylight and with no one to watch. Now, however, the whole camp was astir; the old professor was washing in front of his tent in the tiny modicum of water allowed him for the purpose, boys were hurrying here and there preparing breakfast; and Dick smiled grimly as he noticed that as Junes and Grosman entered the experts' tent they carefully closed the fly behind them.

He looked across at the professor, who had paused in his ablutions to look in the direction of the tent, and now stood, a comical enough

looking object, his face covered in soap-suds, watching for the reappear-
ance of the prospectors.

Dick and he exchanged a glance of intelligence, and Dick took a step
towards the old man, intending to whisper to him the news of what he
had found the day before; but before he could do so there came a shout
from the tent, followed by a volley of oaths and ejaculations, the sound of
a scuffle, and out into the open burst the two prospectors, locked together in a desperate struggle.

"Hound, schwein-hund, robber!" gasped Grosman, as, with his face
purple with rage and exertion he temporarily got the better of his long
and wiry opponent, and bore him back; "scoundrel that you are you
could not play straight even with me! Where are the diamonds hound
where have you hidden them?"

"Yes, where are they? Own up, you thief!" chorused the two experts,
who, pallid and debauched looking, now stood beside the two struggling
men: and Dick now noticed that Gilderman held the small strong box
and that it was open, and empty. The diamonds had gone!

CHAPTER IV

The whole camp had now clustered round the fallen men, the professor grotesque in his thickly lathered face, Dick intensely interested and
enjoying this fall-out among thieves, the experts and financial men
voluble and uneasy.

And still Grosman knelt upon his slighter opponent, and still he
gasped curses and questions; keeping so tight a grip upon Junes' throat
that his eyes were starting from his head and he could scarce breathe,
much less answer.

"Here loosen him a bit!" said Dick, grasping the big man by the
shoulder. "Do you hear? You'll choke the man and how the blazes can he
answer you when you hold him like that? Now then what's the matter?"

"The diamonds are gone," said the glib Gilderman. "We each have a
key on a chain round our necks. They were safe when we went to bed.
The box was locked then now it is open and the stones are gone."

"He has them, the hound," said Grosman, "we had arranged,
schwein- hund," he yelled again, "it was to have been to-morrow night
and you have stolen them from me; where have you buried them?"

"Come off it," said Dick savagely for Junes was again choking and
this time he twisted Grosman's arm till he freed the under man's throat.

"Now then, Junes what have you got to say?"

"Liar and thief himself," gasped the half-choked Junes, "he has taken them while I slept. We had planned . . . Oh! let me up, damn you, and I'll tell them of your plan, you robbing, thieving swine, that can't play straight even with your pal! Let me up, you German hog: let me get a holt on you, and I'll show you. Let me up!"

"Let him up," said Dick, filled with keen enjoyment at seeing these two unprincipled scoundrels mauling each other, and only regretting the fact that the equally rascally onlookers did not take a hand; "let him up, man; give him fair play, and let's hear all about it."

And aided by the strong arm of the still soapy professor, he hauled the furious Grosman off his prey.

And now comedy changed instantly to tragedy, for the panting Junes, springing to his feet, drew his revolver and fired point-blank at his late assailant. Grosman spun half round, his mouth opened in a ghastly grin, and making two staggering steps, he fell to the ground, whilst Junes, profiting by the confusion, sprang to his horse and vaulted into the saddle.

"Hands up," he shouted, covering the group with his revolver. "I shoot the first man who moves. Grosman, you dog, where are the stones?"

The dying man partly raised himself, and fixed an awful gaze upon his murderer. "Murderer and thief!" he gasped, "you have them yourself. I never woke till Sydney shook me!"

"Hell! . . ." said Junes, "I believe you now! There's more roguery here than even I knew of! Hark you, Gilderman, and you other sharks and keep your hands up. Professor, and you, Sydney listen! These other men are thieves all; they've paid us to salt every patch they've tried, so far! They brought over a thousand carats of diamonds stolen from Kolman's Kop to do it with; I know who they bought them from! And Grosman and I thought they deserved to be robbed, and we intended doing so to-night. But one of these swine must have thought of the same game, and hid the stones somewhere. Own up, you cowardly blighters which of you has taken them where are they? Quick! . . . Keep your distance; Sydney this ain't your trouble, and if you move again I'll put a bullet through you," he continued; for Dick was edging near with an idea of making a spring at the armed and desperate man, "and you, professor, help Grosman. ... I'm sorry I shot you now, Heinriech! Now then, I want those diamonds quick, you Jo'burg sharps!"

The four scared men raised their voices in a chorus of protestations, in the middle of which Dick's eye caught sight of something over Junes' shoulder that caused him to start involuntarily. About half a mile away a small cloud of dust was rising. Something or somebody was coming, and quickly too.

Slight as had been Dick's movement, Junes had noted it, and still covering the group, he swung his horse round till he could glance in the direction of the little cloud of dust, through which two horsemen could now be seen; and the glitter of the sun on their rifles showed them to be armed men, probably mounted police.

A bitter curse broke from Junes' pale lips. "Police, by God!" he said; "they're too near or I'd shoot all four of you whining swine. Hell! and I've killed Grosman for nothing!"

And furiously lashing his startled horse he spurred madly away, striking savagely with his sjambok at the cowering quartette as he passed.

"A rifle, a rifle" gasped the wounded man, now plainly dying, and his ghastly face more awful by the look of terrible vindictiveness it now wore "shoot at the horse!"

But before a rifle was forthcoming the two mounted police rode into camp. They were bronzed, burly men, arrayed in a corduroy uniform, with a wide felt hat bearing a large Imperial crown in gilt as a badge, and were fully armed with Mauser rifles, revolver and light saber.

"Donnerwetter!" exclaimed the leader, a big sergeant, or wachtmeister, as they cantered up. "What is this, murder?"

"Murder and there goes the murderer!" said the professor.

"And is it you, Brandt?" he exclaimed, as he looked into the sergeant's face.

"Brandt is my name it is true," said the wachtmeister gruffly, as he peered at the soap-lathered countenance before him, "but who are you? I can see naught but soap. . . . Himmel," he shouted joyfully, as the professor beamed back at him, "I was blind. It is my dear and honored Herr Professor from Munich! Now, Gott sie dank, I see you again after all these years!"

"It is indeed I, Brandt," said the professor, "but spur, man, spur, and bring back that man we must talk later!"

With a sharp word to the trooper, Brandt unslung his rifle and spurred headlong after the fleeing horseman, now rapidly nearing the shelter of the dunes.

Meanwhile, the professor and Dick turned their attention to the dying man, whilst the others resumed the clamor of questions and recriminations which the arrival of the police had interrupted.

Gilderman, his self-confidence almost restored by the approaching death of one, and the flight of the other of his accusers, now tried to brazen matters out.

Thrusting himself before Dick, who was helping dress the wound, he bent down before Grosman and began loudly, so that all might hear.

"Now then, Grosman, where are those diamonds? It is a most outrageous thing that you have done, to rob your employers in this manner. And that ridiculous lie of Junes' about salting! Come, man, tell me where the diamonds are, and tell these people that Junes made up that yarn as you know he did and I'll try to save you from the police. Come now own up where are the stones?"

"You cannot save him from death and the Maker who will judge him," said the professor sternly as he came from his tent with his medicine chest. "Man, think shame to pester the man so; men do not lie on their deathbed"; and as Gilderman did not move he swung him aside by the collar as though he had been a child.

Gilderman uttered a furious exclamation. "Absurd preposterous professor, surely you are not mad enough to believe the story this would-be thief has told?"

"Story?" queried the professor, "what story has he told? Junes, yes! but this man, so far, has accused you of nothing!"

Gilderman flushed with vexation at the false step he had made.

"But the diamonds?" he insisted, "he confessed they had planned to steal them. Make him tell you where they are?"

"Maybe the police will bring them back with Junes," said the professor, going on with his work of dressing the wound. "And if not, you ask? Well, Herr Gilderman, what does it matter, a thousand carats or so! The rich fields you found them on are still there; it took but a few hours to find the stones, surely we can return to those so rich fields and find again a thousand carats! Hein?"

Gilderman answered nothing, but if looks could have killed the old professor, who did not even look at him, and Dick, who grinned maliciously full in his face, both of them would have preceded Grosman.

Just then a faint shot sounded in the direction of the pursuit. It was followed by another and another . . . then a regular fusillade.

"They are kneeling on the top of the first dune," called Jelder from a little rise a few yards away. "Now they are mounting again and coming back."

"Then he's got away," said Dick, "his horse was fresh and they looked as though they had ridden far."

"Curse him, may he roast in hell," whispered the dying man, "but what he said was true."

"Hush," said the professor, "do not try to talk now. Save your breath, man, and tell your story only to the police. And remember I can do but little for you your time is very short."

By this the police came cantering back into camp. "We hit him," said the wachtmeister. "I saw him stagger in the saddle just as he got into the big dunes. His horse was fresh and ours were fagged, it was useless to follow farther. If he is badly hit we shall find him at the waterhole, if not, he will run right into the arms of the patrol we meet there. And now, what is all this about?"

Gilderman took up the tale in voluble German, and it was now evident that, shaken by the protestations of the dying man, and of his murderer, he was now suspicious of Jelder, who had held a key to the box in common with himself. He had been awakened by the outcry that the prospectors made when they saw the empty box lying by the side of the bed. His key he remarked pointedly was still fast round his neck perhaps, he added significantly, Jelder had left his lying about overnight? Jelder flushed angrily, and drawing his key out by the thin gold chain that secured it beneath his vest, shook it in Gilderman's face, when mutual recriminations began without undue loss of time.

The old professor's wine had done its work well in more ways than one.

Their colleagues, Zweiter and Spattboom, instantly took sides, and so they wrangled and vociferated, what time the big German wachtmeister made voluminous notes in a big pocket book.

During all this, the old professor said not a word, though there was a grim twinkle in his eye as he noted the spread of the quarrel.

Aided by Dick, he had now finished attending to the dying man, whom they had taken into the professor's tent, and who lay gasping painfully, with the air whistling through the hole Junes' bullet had made in his lungs. He whispered something hoarsely and painfully to the professor.

"Come, Herr wachtmeister," the latter called to the big sergeant, "the man has but little time, and would make a statement."

The sergeant came and knelt by the dying man. "Where are the diamonds," he asked, pencil in hand.

"Nein, ich wissen nicht," gasped Grosman, "stoop lower, and I will tell all ... I know."

"He lies," said Gilderman and Jelder together, crowding near to the bed. "Herr wachtmeister, why listen to him he lies!"

"Silence," stormed the wachtmeister fiercely, "your time will come to speak, stand back. And how know you if he lies before he speaks? Back!" And he forced them to do so, whilst in short, sobbing gasps, the dying man told of the whole knavery: how they had been bribed to do the actual salting, how each day Gilderman and Jelder had given them a certain number of stones to strew in likely places, and find ostentatiously in sight of the professor, how he and Junes had conceived the idea of stealing the diamonds and burying them where they could find them later, and how, when that morning they had overslept and entered the tent late and seen the strong box lying there empty, each had instantly suspected the other of stealing a march upon him. But dying he, Grosman, swore he knew nothing of the stones nor did he now believe that Junes did!

"Those thieves, those men who first put temptation in our way, they know, ask them, curse them!" he concluded, whilst the sergeant peremptorily demanded silence from the accused men, who were storming angrily at the dying man's denunciation.

"Brietmann," he called to his comrade, "search all the tents everything! I arrest you all, let no man move till a search has been made. Now," he continued, rising from the dying man's side, and turning on them, "which of you has the diamonds?"

"Why should we steal them, why believe the tale of this thief who owns he meant to steal them, why believe him against us?" they demanded, united again now, in their efforts to discredit Grosman.

"One at a time," said the wachtmeister angrily, "and silence, you others." And he proceeded to catechize and badger them one by one, filling page after page of his notebook with their replies.

Meanwhile Brietmann searched tent after tent; ransacking bags, portmanteaux and boxes, shaking out clothing and blankets, and prying into every conceivable article in a vain endeavor to find the stones; whilst the indignant quartette under examination broke out again and again in a storm of impotent wrath.

In the middle of this hubbub the professor's voice was heard for the first time.

"Hush!" he commanded sternly, "in the name of common humanity, hush! at least for a minute. The man is dying."

Even as he spoke, Grosman, the death rattle in his throat, in a last convulsive effort, raised himself on his elbow, and with a terrible look on his face pointed an accusing finger at Gilderman and the group round him, and with a last choking attempt at speech fell back dead.

Immediately Brietmann, who had finished his search in the other tents, and stood looking on, addressed the wachtmeister:

"There is nothing there," he said, "and there remains but this the Herr Professor's tent to search."

The wachtmeister turned apologetically to the professor:

"The Herr Professor will permit?" he asked.

"And why this indignity, Brandt?" demanded the professor sternly.

"It is my duty, Herr Professor; in such cases I may not discriminate," apologized Brandt, "and it is but a matter of form."

"So be it, search!" and the offended professor turned again to the dead man, ignoring the industrious Brietmann, who emptied bags, unlocked boxes, peered into jars of chemicals, and generally upset the scientist's most sacred possessions.

At length, in a dark corner of the tent, Brietmann came to a black box secured with a big padlock.

"Herr Professor," he called; "this box. It is locked."

The professor simply grunted.

"The key, Herr Professor," he persisted.

"I advise you to leave that box alone," growled the owner.

"It must be opened, nicht warum, wachtmeister?" asked Brietmann of the sergeant.

"Ja wohl," said the wachtmeister.

"Again I advise you not," said the old man. "Surely there is no need; I do not wish it opened."

By now every one was looking at the professor with wonder or suspicion, even Dick could not understand his reluctance to have the box opened.

"Sehr gut," said he, as all eyes were turned on him, "take the key!" and he flung it over to where Brietmann knelt by the box.

The policeman fumbled with the lock, threw back the lid, and simultaneously gave vent to a terrific yell, as he flung himself violently backwards. For from the open box rose the writhing forms of half a dozen big cobras, their hoods flattened and arched, vicious and ready to strike, whilst over one of the corners came gliding the broad flattened head and bloated body of a huge puff-adder.

Within five seconds no one remained in the big tent but the dead man and the professor, who, laughing softly, proceeded to collect his straying pets; showing an utter disregard of any danger of being bitten, accountable for by the fact that he had removed every fang from the poisonous specimens long before.

Dick had been as lively as any one in making tracks, for he had a horror of snakes, and as he burst from the tent his foot caught in a guy-rope and down he went with the big wachtmeister sprawling on top of him. Both scrambled up in quick time, for each of them imagined he had snakes crawling all over him, but as Dick rose to his feet, out from the bosom of his shirt fell the red handkerchief full of diamonds he had found the day before, and as it fell out rolled a dozen or more of the little brilliants and lay there flashing and sparkling in the sun- light.

"Donner-wetter!" yelled the wachtmeister, "the diamonds! Here is the thief!" And instantly he seized Dick in a formidable grip.

Curses and execrations burst from the other men, who, wildly excited, crowded round Dick and the diamonds threatening and exulting.

"Thief! Scoundrel! Rascally mule-driver! Schwein-hund!" they cried.

"The handcuffs, Brietmann! Quick!" shouted the sergeant, and Dick realized instantly the seriousness of his position. He had had no opportunity of telling the professor of the find he had made; and who among these rogues each eager to fix the guilt on some one else and discredit the tale both the dead man and Junes had told would believe him if he told the story now?

The quantity of diamonds he had found about equaled the stolen contents of the box, and things could scarcely look blacker for him. He knew the law was likely to be severe with him, as a Britisher he would probably get the extreme sentence. There was no one but the professor to appeal to and, bitter thought, would even he believe him with all this damning evidence against him? All this passed through his mind in an instant, as he stood in amazement, too taken aback to speak, and passively staring at the fallen diamonds.

Then the wachtmeister's grip tightened, as Brietmann hurried up, making ready the handcuffs as he came.

"I did not steal them!" shouted Dick, finding his tongue at last. "I will explain. Professor! Professor! I did not steal them!"

"Lying rogue," said, or rather snarled Gilderman, thrusting his face close to Dick's, and filled with the rage of a lately frightened man. "Filthy donkey-driver and thief you were too miserable and contemptible for us even to suspect!"

And secure in the fact that the wachtmeister held Dick, he struck the latter across the face with his open hand.

Before he had time to draw back things happened.

Dick, blazing with fury at the indignity, wrenched himself free of the wachtmeister, as though that big man had been a child, struck Gilderman a terrific smash on the nose that flattened it and him instantly, and seizing Jelder, who had tried to trip him, he threw that unfortunate Israelite on the top of his colleague. But now the other men flung themselves upon Dick simultaneously, and for a short but crowded period a most memorable scrap took place in and round that little prospecting camp.

Dick, as he afterwards expressed it, was "all out" in that brief but brisk encounter, and fought with every limb and muscle he possessed.

Borne down by sheer numbers for a moment, he succeeded in twisting Brietmann under him, and his knee, judiciously planted in the plump policeman's embonpoint as they fell, with the weight of the other crowd on top of them, drove all the wind out of that unfortunate man, who, for a time, took no further interest in the proceedings.

Dick felt him gasp and subside, and at that very moment his hand came in contact with the heavy steel handcuffs. Here was a weapon worth having, and with such odds against him Dick had no hesitation in using it, and swinging them round blindly at the arms clutching at him, he felt them meet flesh and bone with a soul-satisfying crunch. A sharp yelp followed, and Dick felt the scrum above him lighten, as Zweiter retired from the fray, spitting blood and curses in a polyglot and highly satisfactory manner.

But now the big wachtmeister, a powerful and athletic man, was less cumbered by his would-be helpers, and getting a firm grip on Dick with both arms he gradually forced him down on the unfortunate Brietmann, whilst Spattboom, his one remaining helper, valiantly clung to Dick's frantically kicking legs. With a last desperate effort the latter twisted himself sufficiently to allow his free arm to again swing the handcuffs, and this time they caught the wachtmeister neatly on the nose, setting that organ bleeding profusely, and raising the big Teuton's angry passions to a boiling-over point.

So far, to do him but justice, he had made no attempt to use his revolver, but now, roused by the blow, and furious at the sight of his own blood, he immediately released Dick and drew his weapon.

Dick heard the click of the hammer as he cocked it: heard too the furious "Schwein-hund Englander! I'll shoot you dead for that!" saw the muzzle thrust within a few inches of his head, and shut his eyes.

And as he did so the wachtmeister was hauled back by the shirt collar with terrific force, and flung back on the sand with his neck almost broken, whilst the bullet meant for Dick's brains sang over the neighboring sand-dune. A vigorous kick sent Dick's remaining assailant flying, and he scrambled to his feet to see the professor calmly taking possession of the half-stunned wachtmeister's pistol.

"Enough," he exclaimed, "think shame, Brandt, to shoot an unarmed man! That would be cowardly, and you are no coward! They taught you not such unbillig spiel at the gymnasium at Munich."

"Unarmed!" spluttered the wachtmeister, "he has the handcuffs and my nose is smashed! Herr Professor, you must not stand between me and my prisoner. With all respect, no! Brietmann, you schwein-hund! . . . never have I seen such a dummkopf! . . . Secure him, I say!"

"Hold!" roared the professor, "touch him not till I hear what all this is about. Besides, the man will kill you! Never have I seen a better fighter or a better fight! And fair play he shall have. And explain I saw not the beginning of all this, what has the Herr Sydney done?"

"Done," snarled Gilderman, sidling near, his face bruised and discolored from Dick's first uppercut, "done! why don't you see the thieving hound has stolen the diamonds there they lay they fell from his shirt, the dirty thief!"

Apparently for the first time, the professor's glance fell upon the red handkerchief with the diamonds, and he picked them up, and stood balancing them in his hand and looking from Dick to Gilderman before he replied.

"Professor," began Dick, finding his tongue again; "I am no thief that you can bear witness. I--"

The professor interrupted him with a gesture.

"So," said he slowly, "and it was for this you attacked an unarmed and innocent man?"

"Innocent," spluttered Jelder, "this is too thick! There lie the stones, who took them if he didn't?"

"I did," said the professor.

CHAPTER V

There was silence for a few seconds, except for a universal gasp of wonder, which as far as Dick was concerned was mingled with relief and admiration.

For here was this wonderful old professor, who had already been a surprise packet to Dick in several ways, weighing in with a most finished and artistic lie, just in the nick of time to save him when everything appeared lost!

"You!" cried Gilderman, as the professor stood, still holding Brandt's revolver, and smiling blandly at the group of mauled and discomfited scoundrels; "You?"

"Yes!" he thundered, his jaw setting sternly again. "I, I, who you thought to dupe. I, who have seen through your perfidious plan from the first ('Oh, oh!' thought Dick, 'that's for the benefit of the police.') I, who you would have made the scapegoat for your villainy at the cost of my name and honor I took the stones.

"Come, Herr wachtmeister, take your revolver and listen. There is no need for further concealment. I drugged these men last night, and took the stones foreseeing clearly that these scoundrels would quarrel when the loss was discovered and they realized that they could salt no more nor take back the lying 'proof' they relied upon for their scheme. And it fell out as I had believed though I did not foresee that murder would be done before I could prevent it. . . . And I gave them to the Herr Sydney to guard for me for he was the only honest man among this crowd of scoundrels and I am an old and feeble man!"

The big wachtmeister rubbed his throttled throat feelingly, and grunted dissent, whilst the accused and desperate quartette broke into angry protestations.

"Deny it as you like," said the professor, "Grosman swore it with his dying breath, Junes swore it after he had shot him, Sydney saw the salting with his own eyes."

"The word of a murderer, a delirious man, and a thief against that of four gentlemen!" Gilderman exclaimed, bluffing desperately for the benefit of the wachtmeister and Brietmann; who had pulled themselves together, and stood looking with lowering brows from one to the other.

"Gentlemen! Lieber Gott! Then gentlemen, if you still persist in your innocence, it is but of the simplest thing for you to prove it. The Herr wachtmeister will take us all back to Luderitzbucht, and on the way, what is simpler than to again test the rich spots from which you obtained so easily these thousand carats, hein? If you found these there there will be others, nicht warum? And then I will say that I am sorry! And meanwhile the wachtmeister can keep the stones. And I will answer for this last 'theft' I, whose name is worth more than a thousand such 'gentlemen' as these! And now, Herr wachtmeister or rather shall I say my dear pupil of the old Muenchener days? I regret that I have hurt your throat, but I am sure you would rather that, than be guilty of shooting an innocent and unarmed man who, I am sure, was first assaulted by these gentlemen."

"Ja wohl," grumbled the wachtmeister; "that is true, that coward there struck him after I had seized his arms. Aber donner-wetter, Herr Professor, why not have told me this there in the tent long ago? It would have saved me a broken nose from this 'innocent, unarmed' Englander of yours, and an almost broken neck from yourself! Tausend! I remember that grip of yours in the gymnasium of old! Lieber Gott! but the years have not weakened it. And with this devil incarnate of an Englander to aid you, what had you to fear from six such as these? Why did you not bundle the whole lot back and have them locked up?"

"They were all armed, and we were not," said the professor.

"Then we will disarm them," said Brandt, and covering them with his revolver he made Brietmann do so taking away the revolver that each man carried, and taking not the slightest notice of their protests.

"And now you are under arrest," he told them, "and at any attempt to escape you will be shot."

Then blowing a whistle, he summoned the camp boys who, in mortal fear of the police, had obeyed their first order to remain with the horses some distance away; and who would have seen the white men kill each other till none were left, before daring to disobey that order and told them harshly to bury Grosman, and prepare to strike camp and trek immediately.

Dick, who had stood as one in a dream, and let the professor do all the talking, now shook himself together sufficiently to hand over the handcuffs to Brietmann who only glared at him and apologized to Brandt for the unlucky blow he had given him.

"I bear no malice, friend Englander," said the wachtmeister, "but you have broken my nose. And some day I should like to meet you in friendly ringen-spiel, I think I would pay you in full for that blow!"

"Nothing would suit me better," said Dick eagerly, for he regretted the blow almost, but not quite, as much as the wachtmeister, and he was a past master at wrestling. "Whenever you like, Herr Brandt; shall we try a fall now?"

"Himmel, no!" said the big fellow, "I have had plenty for one day if you have not. We must postpone the pleasure."

Dick set about the business of striking camp, and for a time was fully occupied. Meanwhile his mind was in a whirl. That the professor had invented a plausible lie on the spur of the instant to save him, was of course obvious; but it was apparently not all lie, for he had certainly drugged the wine the previous evening!

But the stones, who had got them? He could have sworn that Junes had told the truth as he rode away murderer though he was! And Grosman, would a dying man lie?

He was itching to get near the professor alone, to tell him his own story, possibly the old man believed him to be the thief although he had lied to save him.

Altogether the whole thing was a puzzle. Meanwhile he went on with his work. Tents were struck, packs made up, and pack animals laden, and soon all that remained of the camp was the trestle, on which, covered with a sheet, lay the still form of Grosman. The wachtmeister sang out a brief order, two of the Hottentots rapidly shoveled out a shallow grave in the sand, barely covering the murdered man. Dick stood by with his hat off he had barely escaped a bullet himself but an hour before!

"Poor beggar," he thought, "shot and buried like a dog, and all because these bigger scoundrels tempted him to run crooked. And he was some woman's son, someone will mourn him. Buried like a dog!"

But it was not so; for looking up he saw the professor, bareheaded, standing beside the grave, prayer-book in hand; and he stood silent and respectful whilst the old man read a short solemn prayer for the dead in his native German.

Then mounting their horses they trotted after the already moving cavalcade, leaving the forlorn little mound and the dead ashes of the camp fire alone marking where their camp had stood.

The police officers rode ahead, the four conspirators, silent and dejected, a short distance behind them, and Dick and the professor brought up the rear. Gradually they fell farther behind, till well out of earshot of the others, and Dick at last had the chance to tell the story of how he found the stones.

"Professor," he began, in low eager tones, "I cannot thank you enough for inventing that story to save me. But you must not think I am a thief! These are not the stones from the box I did not steal them."

"I know that," interrupted the professor, "but where got you these?"

"This side the big dune where I first saw Grosman salting two days ago. They lie there in thousands. I got these in an hour or so."

"Now Gott sie Dank!" said the professor joyfully. "These rascals then have too clever been, and the ground is in truth rich! Gott sie Dank! Our trip has not been in vain. But neither the police nor these knaves must know . . . and we must ride on quick. For I bade them test the ground again where they salted and that is the first place, and they must find nothing."

"We are nearly there," said Dick, "and it's risky. For where they salted is barely 300 yards from where the stones lie thick. But we must take them to where they picked their own up and they won't search far they are too down at mouth for that. But, professor, where are the real stones? Who stole them? Who has them?"

"Ach, that is the mystery," replied the professor, and spurred his horse on before Dick could ask him any more.

An hour later they came to the big dune, the scene of Grosman's salting, and here Dick, with mixed feelings, stood by whilst Gilderman made his last attempt at bluff setting the boys to work with sieves, whilst he and his colleagues searched all around the vicinity of that last "rich find," and, of course, finding nothing; whilst had he known it, but a bare stone's throw or two away they were lying in abundance.

Dick could almost have found it in his heart to pity him, as the despairing, cadaverous wretch at length gave up the hopeless search.

Late that evening, as they approached the first waterhole, the wachtmeister pointed significantly to a saddled horse cropping quietly near by, whilst as they got nearer the pits, five or six big vultures flapped lazily away. "I knew I hit him," said the wachtmeister significantly.

"Junes," thought Dick; "now if they find he really has the stones what will happen then?"

Junes it was: they found all that the vultures had left of him lying there by the water, with a ghastly bullet-hole through back and shoulder. The marvel was that he had lived to ride so far. But there were no diamonds, and Dick was more mystified than ever. A few pencilled words, scrawled on the leaf of a pocket-book, again telling the tale of the salting and naming Gilderman as the chief conspirator, lay pinned to the dead man's shirt, and the wachtmeister, as he read it, called out grimly to them to come and look at another piece of their work.

Reluctantly they came closer to the awful thing that had once been Junes, whilst the police sergeant, long since inured to such sights all too frequent in the desert read aloud the note, and asked them if they still denied the testimony of the two dead men. Gilderman in vain endeavoured to brazen it out, and the wachtmeister, changing his tactics, forced him and the others to look close at what had been a face, and identify it as that of Junes.

The terrible plan succeeded, for at the gruesome sight, the little bravado left in them gave way entirely. Gilderman, physically sick, staggered away a yard or two and fell in a faint, and Jelder, whimpering like a child, broke down utterly. "Gott in Himmel," he cried, "what a death! I can't stand any more of this! Yes, it is true we were all in it, but the plan was Gilderman's."

Again the wachtmeister made notes; and in their efforts to stand in as well as possible, each now tried to further implicate the other, till the sergeant closed his book and roughly bade them be silent, and keep their precious tale for the Richter in Windhuk, who would try them.

As they rode into Luderitzbucht a week later, one of the first men that Dick saw was Solly, who in the excitement of the past few weeks he had almost forgotten the existence of. But as he saw the little Jew, who had stood by him before and who had been instrumental in getting him his job, he remembered that Solly would expect a full account of all that had happened, and the question was should he tell him of the stones he had found, or only of the salting?

However, he had neither time nor opportunity to say anything then, for encountering the little cavalcade just as the wachtmeister led it up to the police station, he opened his little twinkling eyes wide at the sight of the four dejected and most obvious prisoners, gave Dick a wink which expressed volumes, and made off in a bee line towards the telegraph station. There he sent a most innocent wire to a small retail tobacconist in Kimberley a wire that apparently conveyed nothing more than a complaint as to the quality of certain cigars that Solly had received. Strangely enough, however, within an hour or two of its receipt certain gentlemen vitally connected with diamonds and all concerned in them knew that they had no reason to fear the great "North-Eastern" diamond fields, as they had been salted.

Meanwhile the wachtmeister handed over Gilderman and Co. to the officer in charge at the police station, where they were detained in common with the diamonds--Dick's diamonds!

To the Herr Professor the officials were politeness itself, and thanks to his good offices even Dick was treated with civility Englishman though he was.

As they left the station they met the company's Luderitzbucht agent, a most important gentleman, who was looking both flushed and perturbed. It was evident that news travelled quickly in Luderitzbucht, for he had already as his first words clearly proved heard of the arrests.

"Herr Professor," he blurted out, "what a calamity! Most unfortunate. Gilderman and the others all arrested. Surely most tactless! Could it not have been avoided? It might have been explained, but to arrest them all! The company is as good as floated."

"Not all," said the professor grimly, looking the excited agent up and down. "Not all, Herr Hauptmann, two are dead. We caught them Salting, Herr Sydney here and myself, surely it was 'tactless' of them? A calamity! Truly yes, for them! And, Herr Hauptmann, if the new 'company' has been floated without waiting for my report, so much the worse for them."

The agent glared from the professor to Dick, as though he would have liked to eat both of them, but he saw he had made a mistake, also saw that the thousand shares Gilderman had promised him would never materialize, and changed his tactics.

"My dear Herr Professor," he said, "of course you were right. I was so upset for a moment that I did not quite know how to look at it, but of course you are right. And the ground then is worthless, is it not so?"

"I would not go so far as to say that," said the professor, cautiously; "there has been no real test these rascals started their salting at once. I leave immediately for Johannesburg to-night. I hear there is a steamer leaving then and there I shall report thoroughly on what has happened. Possibly the company will send up a more carefully chosen expedition again, they have the option for another three months. In that case, and if they wish me to return, the Herr Sydney here will take charge of the prospecting."

The agent looked sourly at Dick. "You know, professor, the company like to engage their own prospectors," he demurred.

"Yes, and I believe last time you recommended one of them," replied the professor blandly. "Last time the company made a colossal mistake, prospectors, experts, representatives, all were rogues! Two lie dead back there in the dunes and four lie in gaol! I want no more of that kind. And, Herr Hauptmann, if I go, this man goes, if there is a man in the country who can find diamonds there, it is he."

"That's a fact," said Dick to himself, as he realized all the professor was doing for him.

"And now, Herr Hauptmann," continued the old man, as they reached the agent's office, "pay Sydney his cheque and double it, I will answer to the company."

So Dick got his cheque, and his discharge, and making a straight line for the bank he changed the former, without loss of time. He had seen cheques stopped before, and trusted Hauptmann just about as much as he had trusted the Gilderman outfit.

Then he went to the hotel, where the professor's belongings had been dumped in the biggest room the building boasted.

Here the scientist called him in, and locking the door, sat down on the bed and looked at him.

"Young and strong, and honest, you should become rich in this country, where honest men are so scarce," he said kindly. "Herr Sydney, or rather do I call you Dick, for you are young enough to be my son, you heard what I told the agent? Well, I go to Johannesburg in a few hours, but I shall come back, I am sure, though whether the company sends me straight back, or whether they await the expiration of the syndicate's lease, I cannot say, financiers do strange things, and who knows what they will do?"

"But when I come, you go too, and there will be an opportunity for you such as few men have. You will know for certain beforehand where the stones lie rich, you can purchase shares as soon as flotation is effected, knowing well they will become valuable, you can make your fortune."

"But I have no money," said Dick, "my cheque won't last long."

"You see that box," asked the professor, pointing to a certain black, padlocked trunk amongst his baggage.

"I haven't forgotten it," said Dick feelingly.

"Well, the wherewithal to pave your way to fortune lies in that."

"Snakes!" exclaimed Dick, with a lively recollection of the last time that box had been opened.

The professor moved towards it. Dick moved towards the door.

"Wait, man, wait!" said the professor. "But they are harmless."

"Oh, yes! I know," said Dick, edging still nearer the door. "Pretty little things, some people call them, like that scorpion you raved about, before! Here, I say, professor, play the game; I don't want fortunes of that kind here, I'm off!"

"The door is locked," said the old man calmly; "Wunderbahr! here is a man I thought feared nothing, a fighter of the best, afraid of a few harmless snakes!"

"Professor," pleaded Dick, as the old man bent over the padlock, "don't do it; I don't want any fortune. Oh, Lord! I shall have two fits! Yow! Help! there he goes!" and as the box opened Dick sprang on to the bed.

"Quite harmless," said the professor, as he flung back the lid; "and but how splendid, wunderschoen, hein? Three new specimens among them of varieties quite unknown, and the fame will be mine. And the scorpion you discovered, and so generously gave me! Ach, meine freund, now I can indeed repay you for your so great generosity. See, then!" And with a dramatic gesture he plunged his hand down among the wriggling snakes, and groping among them in a manner that made every hair on Dick's head stand up till he felt like a porcupine, he drew forth a small bundle, and tossed it on the bed.

"Open it," he ordered. "No! dummkopf! there are no snakes in it open!"

Dick's fingers trembled as he undid the knots, he knew by the feel what to expect.

Yes, there they were, the thousand carats of diamonds that had caused two violent deaths and a heap of trouble already, a double handful of beautiful little sparkling gems; the very facsimile of those others that Dick had found and that now lay locked up and confiscated at the police-station.

"They are yours," said the professor. "Whose, if not? Gilderman's or those other scoundrels in gaol? The company's? It has no rights on the fields yet! The Government's? It has those others you found in place of these, and to attempt to explain now would bring complications, and maybe, who knows, place us both in gaol!"

Dick was tempted, but demurred.

"You see, professor," he said reluctantly, "these are not my stones. It isn't as if they were the stones I really found!"

"The police will scarcely give you those, I repeat," answered the other. "Lieber Gott, man, say what you mean! I stole them, is that it? Of course I did, as I had a perfect right to, to bring about what I did, the confession of these knaves; and but that Brandt annoyed me with his insistence to search my tent I should have told him then. As it was, I let that fool Brietmann search, knowing that he would be frightened when he opened the box. Ach, you brave men! And then, Dick, Herr Sydney, if you wish? Well, Dick then, what would have happened to you if they had found the diamonds you had? Just was I in time to make up the tale I did when I saw you righting on the ground with the wachtmeister's pistol at your head! Soh if you will, I stole them. Will you not take them from me? They had yours in place of them; take them, they are yours. And the one big director of the company in Johannesburg, to whom I shall the truth tell, he will applaud what I have done."

The professor's arguments were far from flawless, but Dick yielded; for it had seemed more than hard to see the diamonds he had himself found handed over to the police and after all, it did not seem right to let a thousand carats of diamonds go begging for an owner!

And whatever qualms he had vanished at the delight of the old professor, as he made up the parcel again and stowed it carefully away in his pocket.

An hour later the professor went on board, and Dick beat up a few friends, most of whom were dead broke, and proceeded to the Europatia Hof, the leading hotel, where he ordered such a feast as made the manager promptly ask for payment in advance.

Satisfied on that point, he proceeded to surpass himself, in so far as the limited capabilities of Luderitzbucht were concerned, and that night Dick and four other hungry men made up for lost time. The food was good, and the champagne that washed it down excellent, and Dick, as he bade the other men "Good-night," and turned away from the hotel towards his old diggings, felt at peace with all mankind. He had still twenty pounds in his pocket, he had the professor's promise of leading another trip to the north-east; and above all, he had a thousand carats of diamonds tied tightly in a bundle made fast inside his shirt.

Fortune was smiling again, and full of happy dreams for the future he sauntered down the pitch dark street towards his room, whistling, and without a care. And as he reached the door something struck him with a dull, heavy thud at the back of the head, and he fell like a log on his own door-step.

When he came to himself it was still dark, and for a moment he could scarce remember what had happened. Then it all came back to him in a flash; he had been sandbagged. His money was gone to the last penny, and so were the diamonds.

Faint and sick, he dragged himself into his room and bathed his aching head; and now he saw, too, that all his belongings had been ransacked. "They waited for me, here," he thought, and he groaned in bitterness of spirit as he realized that as far as the diamonds were concerned it was useless to try and obtain redress legally, he had had no right to their possession!

The professor had gone, there was no one he could turn to, yes, there was Solly.

And as soon as it was light he went and found him of course still in bed!

"Ah," he said, "I heard you was having a thick night, and you look like it. Blued your cheque, I suppose?"

"Not all," said Dick, "but it's gone!" And he told him everything.

"Blazes!" exclaimed the little man, leaping from his bed and beginning to dress in mad haste. "You fathead, you've done a fine thing. Why, you let me believe the fields were salted!"

"They were," said Dick, "but the real stones were there all the same!"

"But, you loony, I should have known this at once! Why, I went straight and wired to the people who must know these things; the people who make or break all diamond ventures! My people!"

"The Johannesburg Company that sent the professor?" asked Dick, in his innocence.

"Johannesburg, the professor! I don't think!" said Solly with the greatest scorn. "No, the people that control diamonds are . . . a little firm of tobacconists in Kimberley!"

3.   THE FOLLOWER

In a desolate and lonely spot near the wide expanse of mud-flats which form the mouth of the Orange River there stands the roofless ruin of an old farm-house. Its stone walls, of huge thickness, and the high stone kraal with huge iron hinges only remaining where once swung a formidable door, speak eloquently of the time when this remote part of Klein Namaqualand, in common with the islands and lower reaches of the Orange River, was infested with bands of Hottentot outlaws and robbers, and when the daring white man who had ventured among them kept his scant flocks and herds under lock and key, and guarded them with a strong hand.

To the south, towards Port Nolloth, stretches seventy-odd miles of desolate, waterless sand-scrub; eastward lie vast expanses of similarly dreary, featureless, undulating scrub, beyond which rise the unknown and mysterious mountains of the Richtersfeld and hundreds of miles of uninhabited country; westward is the wide lonely ocean; and to the north, across the Orange River, lie the dreaded sand-dunes of German South-West Africa.

It was in the direction of the dunes, gleaming vague and silver-white in the clear moonlight, that the eyes of the three white men prospectors who had forgathered in this lonely spot were turned as they sat, finishing their evening meal, beside a bright fire that lit up the broken and roofless walls. They had met after months of lonely wanderings: Sidney and Ransford amongst the mountains of the Richtersfeld, Jason from long and arduous expeditions along the Great Fish River and amongst the trackless sands across the river. The talk had been of the dunes; of men lost and dying of thirst a few miles from camp; of terrific storms that lifted the sand in huge masses, and whirled it across the land, over-whelming all it encountered; of whole dunes that were shifted by the wind, leaving gruesome things disclosed in the hollows where once they had stood; of diamonds, danger and death.

"Yes!" said Jason, "there's many a man been lost since the diamond rush first started: gone away from camp and never turned up again died of thirst most of them, of course, though I daresay the Bushmen ac-counted for some. Sometimes the sand has overwhelmed them and buried their bodies for ever. Sometimes after a big storm it gives up its dead as the sea does. I've seen some queer things there myself. Once near Easter Cliffs, after a terrific storm had shifted all the dunes, I came across the bodies of a dozen white men, all together and mummified and wonderfully preserved. God knows how they died and how long they'd been there!

"But the weirdest thing that ever happened to me up there was when Carfax disappeared. You remember Carfax? A tall, bony, powerful chap he was, quiet and dour, and with a strong vein of superstition in him. Anyhow, he was a good prospector and a reliable man, and when the rush for the northern fields took place about two years ago. He was one of a party of four of us who had been landed with a few kegs of water and bare necessities on the waterless coast opposite Hollams Bird Island. Here we searched in vain for diamonds, the dunes being exceptionally difficult and the wind that came up every afternoon converting the whole country into a whirling chaos that it was impossible to see in, or work in next to impossible to exist in.

"On the third evening, after an exceptionally strong gale had nearly choked, blinded, and overwhelmed us, Carfax did not turn up in camp, and though we searched all the following day we found no trace of him not a vestige; for one of the worst things about the dunes is that when the wind is blowing the spoor is filled up almost immediately with drifting sand; though peculiarly enough a day or two later the spoor will show again, when the light sand has again been blown out. He had only a small water-bottle with him, the heat was like Hades itself, and we all thought he was dead.

"But on the second night of his absence I shall never forget it the wind had gone down completely, and the long stretches of white dunes lay clear and bright in the white moonlight. The other fellows lay asleep on the sand, exhausted, for we had had a terrible day, but I couldn't sleep I never can in bright moonlight.' And after tossing around for some time I got up, lit a pipe, and walked over to the water-barrel to get a drink. Poor Carfax was still in my mind, and I stood thinking of him and gazing out in the direction in which he had gone, straining my eyes in the forlorn hope of seeing something moving; but the dead silver-white of the sand dunes was unbroken by a single speck.

"I stood thus for some time, and was turning once more towards the others when a faint movement in the vague distance caught my eye. Yes! something or some one was crossing the ridge of a big dune in my direction! A jackal maybe! No, it was too big for that; the faint form was certainly that of a man or were there two? I didn't wait longer, but, running back and grabbing a water bottle, I started off at a run towards whoever it was.

"Moonlight is puzzling sometimes, and I could scarcely make out if there was one figure or two: one seemed to follow the other at a little distance. But as I got nearer I could see it was Carfax alone. 'Carfax! Carfax!' I called out, 'thank God you're alive we'd given you up!' He made no answer, but came on slowly and falteringly, turning repeatedly as though to gaze behind. Now I saw that he was in the last stage of exhaustion: his face was drawn and ghastly, and his cracked and swollen lips were moving rapidly in broken, incoherent words; his sufferings had plainly driven him out of his mind. He snatched at the water bottle and drained it at a draught; then, clutching me by the arm, he pointed back across the dunes.

"'There! there! see! he follows me always, since I found the diamonds! Look! look!'

"As he pointed his face was ghastly with fear, and I too looked back, expecting to see I knew not what. Was he followed, and by whom? I had thought at first there had been one following; but no, there was nothing to be seen. Who could be following him in this desolate place? But still he clutched my arm, and gibbered, and pointed back, and now my eyes were playing tricks again: surely there was a shadow! No, there was nothing there no human being at any rate. Possibly it had been a jackal. So, soothing him as best I could, I helped the poor demented fellow back to camp, he with many a backward look of fear, and I myself with an uncanny feeling that we were being followed.

"Well, he was delirious for days; and when the cutter came back to pick us up and take us to another spot farther up the coast he was too ill to be moved, so we rigged up a bit of a tent and I was left to nurse him till the boat returned again. It was a weird experience, alone in that desolate spot with a madman for company; for though he quieted down after the others had gone he still had the hallucination of being followed and watched; and especially in the night, when I wanted to sleep, he would seize me by the arm and point through the tent door to the bright moonlight outside. 'There! there!' he would mutter, 'don't you see him? look at his square-toed boots and brass buckles. See how his ghastly dead eyes glare! Keep him from me, Jason; keep him from me; he shall not have them back; he has been dead hundreds of years; keep him from me they are mine!' And in my overstrung, nervous state I could have sworn on one or two occasions that I too saw such a figure.

"He gradually got calmer and more himself, and then he told me a strange tale of what had happened to him in the dunes.

"He had been overtaken by a sandstorm many miles from the camp, and had struggled on till absolutely exhausted, not daring to lie down to rest lest the fast whirling sand should overwhelm him; and when late at night the wind had fallen he was hopelessly and utterly lost, and had thrown himself down in a sheltered spot deep hollowed out by the wind between two gigantic dunes, and had at once fallen into the deep sleep of exhaustion.

"Then he had dreamed a startling and vivid dream that had seemed half reality. He saw three men come down over the big dune to close beside where he lay rough-looking men in a costume of long ago, with cocked hats, broad breeches, and buckled shoes; and the moonlight shone on the brass hilts of their cutlasses and pistols. They took no notice of him, but, stooping, began to pick up the bright diamonds that Carfax now saw covered the sand before them. Soon the bag they held was full and a quarrel arose; for he saw two of the men draw their swords and fight fiercely, whilst the other, a tall hawk-faced man, stood by and watched, holding the bag. At length one fell, pierced through by the other's broad blade; and as the victor stood over him the hawk-faced man cut him down from behind, and stood, laughing horribly and holding the bag of diamonds before their dying eyes. And as he laughed one of them, with a last effort, drew a pistol from his belt and shot him dead.

"At the report the scene vanished, and Carfax awoke with a start. The dream had been so vivid that the pistol-shot seemed still to be ringing in his ears, and he sprang to his feet, scarcely knowing what he should see. The air was clear of dust now, and the moon shone brightly; and by its light he saw a few paces from him a prostrate form partly covered in sand. He bent over it: it was the body of a man, a man dressed in a strange old-world costume a dead man, dead hundreds of years, and mummified and wonderfully preserved by the sands that had covered him deep through the centuries, until the big gale of yesterday had lifted the heavy pall. Huddled near by lay two other indistinct forms; and Carfax, his dream still vividly before him, knew well what they were.

"Yes! there too lay the leather bag at his feet! And trembling with excitement he knelt and plunged his hand into it, and drew out a handful of big, dully gleaming diamonds. And as he gazed at the treasure his wrist was clutched in an icy grasp, and turning in terror he found the horrible eyes of the dead man glaring close into his own.

"With a scream of horror he wrenched away his wrist, and, still clutching the stones, fled madly across the dunes, pursued by the fearful figure of the long-dead man. Stumbling, falling, on and on he fled, till the moon paled and the stars faded and the bright sun rose and gave the hunted man a gleam of courage; but his fearful glance behind him still showed the grim figure of he who followed.

"He could not tell what instinct had guided him back to camp; but all through that awful day he had stumbled on through the roasting heat of the dunes, till late at night when I had seen him and gone to meet him as I described.

"All this he told me that night in the tent, now and again starting and glancing fearfully out and across the sands to point out the dread watcher he believed hovered near him. I tried to soothe him, to laugh away his fears, to tell him it was all a dream. And then? Well, he fumbled in his shirt and drew forth a little package tied up in a rag, and with many a fearful glance his trembling fingers undid it, and there poured forth a little cascade of magnificent diamonds far finer than anything I had ever seen before or since in German West: a fortune in fact! I sat astounded, for I had not dreamed of this. Where they came from there must be more a fortune for us all! Then I found my tongue. 'Carfax, man,' I said, 'this is wonderful! Can you find your way back? It will make us all rich.' He shuddered. 'No! no!' he said, his hand pressed to his eyes as though to shut out a scene of horror; 'he is there! No, he cannot be; he is watching here for me he will follow me always! Oh! Jason, don't leave me alone, old man; don't leave me; we'll get away together when the boat comes! there's enough for us both! don't leave me!'

"After a time he sank into a troubled sleep; but to me sleep was now out of the question. Where on earth had he found the diamonds? They, at least, were real. Had he really found a spot where the terrific gale had shifted the sand and laid bare a treasure and tragedy of long ago? Such things might be. I had seen dead men in the dunes myself, and the overwrought state of Carfax, due to his sufferings, would account for the rest. If only he could find his way back when he came to his proper senses again.

"Thus musing I paced up and down outside the tent in the bright moonlight. Carfax was still sleeping, but uneasily, and muttering a lot in his sleep. There across the dunes the diamonds must be there some-where. He had come from yonder towards the big dune. And almost mechanically my footsteps wandered away from the tent towards where I had met Carfax. Here was the spot, here was the place where he had half scared me with his weird story of being followed, and where I had half believed myself that I had seen the follower. Here, for the wind had once more blown the sand from out the filled-in footprints, were our spoors mine meeting his; here we turned back; but what was this? Whose spoor was this, that followed upon our own, back towards where the tent stood!

"My hair rose on my head as I looked. The ghastly white moonlight showed the other spoor quite plainly the print of a broad, square-toed, low-heeled shoe.

"Every man of us wore veldtschoens: there was not a heel among the four of us, and as I marveled and superstitious fear crept upon me there came scream after scream of terror from the direction of the tent; and as I looked, Carfax, barefoot as he had slept, came flying from the tent, his ghastly face contorted with horror, glancing behind him as he ran, and holding out his arms as though to ward off a pursuer.

"Past me he flew, straight across the sand towards the dunes from which he had lately come, his shrieks getting fainter and fainter as he sped until they ceased, and the faint breeze that heralded the dawn brought back the sound of mocking laughter.

"Fear held possession of me, for something had passed me in pursuit of the haunted man, and with terror gripping my faculties, I scarce dared turn my eyes to where the fresh spoor of Carfax's naked feet showed in the sand. Yes! It was there: a heavy, broad, square-toed print following and treading over Carfax's own and showing the signs of a mad pursuit.

"Did I follow them? No! I'm not ashamed to say I did not at any rate not then. Instead, I walked down to the shore, where the solemn breakers offered some sort of companionship, and prayed for morning to come and blot out the ghastly moon and all it had shown me, and save my reason.

"The sun came at last, and with it an awful hurricane that equaled that of the previous week, and I was hard put to it to save our few belongings from being swept away and from being myself overwhelmed. In the evening came the calm, and with it the boat; and, thank God! I had not to face the moonlight again alone.

"Yes, we searched; but the storm had changed the whole aspect of the dunes, and the spoors lay buried under many feet of sand, and well, Carfax was never seen again!"

Jason ended his narrative abruptly, and, rising, lit his pipe with an ember from the dying fire and stood gazing across the river to where the vague mysterious dunes of German West showed silver-white beyond the farther bank. "Good country to be out of!" he said with a shiver. "Come, boys, you'd better turn in. I can't sleep when there's a moon."

4. THE PROOF

The chance was too good to be missed. For days past the baboons had been extremely troublesome killing and mutilating the pick of our milch goats, which had strayed afield in search of food; tearing to pieces the poor mongrel puppy that had been unwise enough to follow them; and even ransacking our tent during the few hours we had left it without a guard. The troop was a large one, and included some of the biggest baboons I had ever seen; but though daring at times, they were exceedingly wary, and amidst the labyrinth of broken country which at the spot hemmed in the Orange River they had hitherto evaded our attempts at retaliation. And now by sheer luck we had stumbled upon them. Jason and I, following up some copper indications amongst the mountain peaks, had turned an abrupt corner and found ourselves within a hundred yards of their big leader a huge grey monster that stood sentinel-wise upon a high rock watching us. The tiny black head of my foresight showed plainly against the wide grey chest of the big brute; I pressed the trigger; and the soft-nosed "303 sped true to the mark. The long hairy arms were flung aloft in a gesture too human to be pleasant, and with a spasmodic spring in the air the baboon fell head- long from the rock, whilst at the report the whole troop, with a chorus of angry, sharp, staccato barks, fled round the shoulder of the mountain and disappeared.

"I hate shooting them," I said, turning to Jason for the first time since we had sighted them; "they're too human altogether, still Hullo, Jason, what's the matter?"

Jason's usually calm, inscrutable face was absolutely convulsed with strong feeling: fear, hatred, loathing what was it? He started as though from a dream.

"God! How I hate them!" he muttered hoarsely. "It was not far from here."

He shouldered his rifle and turned back abruptly towards the camp. I did not attempt to stop him; for though the staunchest friend and comrade, he was of a peculiar disposition; and I knew that he would, if he wanted to do so, tell me his story when the mood suited him. I walked over to the fallen baboon, which lay dead, grim, and hideous, with its chest shattered by my bullet and its formidable fangs bared in a ghastly grin.

That night by the camp-fire, Jason, who had scarcely uttered a syllable in the meanwhile, told me his weird story; but let him tell it in his own words.

"The first chapter of my story began twenty years ago. I had just returned from a shooting and trading trip in Damaraland which had ended in a stiff bout of fever, and was kicking my heels in Cape Town, when one day I received a note from the Curator of the Museum asking me if I would care to act as guide to two gentlemen who wished to follow up the Orange River from its mouth and possibly proceed up the then almost unknown Fish River into Damaraland. I did not care about going back, for my recent trip had been a very rough one; but I was heartily sick of Cape Town, and so I went round to the hotel where the two men were staying, taking the note which the Curator had sent me. 'They don't want to trade or prospect,' he had written me, 'the trip is simply for scientific purposes. Hector Montrose is an ethnologist of wide repute, and he wishes to study the race characteristics of the Hottentots and Bushmen. He is a brilliant disciple of Darwin, too, and has spent a lot of time and money on several trips to the interior of Borneo and other remote spots in search of the so-called "missing link;" and he is, I know, extremely anxious to get near some of those huge baboons that are said to exist along the Orange River. His brother John is quite different, and as long as he is with his brother and there's plenty to shoot he's happy anywhere.'

"I rather expected to meet a couple of old fossils, but to my agreeable surprise I found John and Hector Montrose both younger men than myself and I was under thirty then. Fine young fellows they were too, nearly of an age, and as much alike as two peas. Of medium size, well-knit, and muscular, they were exactly the type of man for a rough trip such as that which we were soon planning. For all my scruples went by the board within ten minutes of our first meeting, and I fell absolutely under the spell and charm of their virile personalities. Splendid chaps, both of them: I never met their like. I can see them now as they sat listening to me. I discussed the trip, and described the kind of country we should have to cover. Their dark, keen, eager faces were so absolutely alike that, except when they laughed, I could scarce tell which was which. Hector, the elder, had had the whole of his front teeth so stopped and plated with gold dentistry that there was but little ivory to be seen, and when he laughed this gave him a strange and rather unpleasing appearance.

"Within a week we were on the veld, and two months later were within fifty miles of where we are sitting now farther up the Orange, where the Great Fish River runs into the larger stream. It is a wild and desolate spot to-day, and there are hippo still on the islands, but twenty years back scarce a white man had ever seen it! We had followed the Orange from its mouth in a leisurely, dawdling manner, spending a few days, or perhaps a week, at those few spots where we found Hottentots or Bushmen. The elder brother seemed to comprehend these wild men by intuition, and the extraordinary 'click' language which I had long since despaired of ever learning seemed to him the simplest thing on earth. Day after day he conversed with them more and more, until his mastery of both tongues was complete. The natives looked up to him as a sort of god, and if he had allowed it would have worshipped him. Hour after hour he would sit conversing with them and questioning them, taking copious notes all the time and gathering from their folklore, legends, traditions, and beliefs; and every day, as he became more engrossed, his brother and I saw less of him. John and I had plenty of sport, for the country teemed with game in those days; but after a time, as Hector grew more and more engrossed in the natives, until he rarely spoke to us, John became anxious, and at last spoke to me. 'Look here, Jason,' he said one day when we were miles from camp after klipbok for the pot, 'I don't like the way Hector's going at all! He scarcely ever speaks now, and he's so queer when he does talk. He wanders in his sleep a lot, and last night he kept on all night talking the most abject nonsense about proving to the world that Darwin was right in his theory of evolution. It's some yarn these infernal Bushmen have told him, I suppose. I wish something would crop up to divert his thoughts in another direction.'

"Well, something happened only too soon. One day, in passing through a narrow ravine, we came suddenly at close quarters with a troop of the biggest baboons I have ever seen. They looked and grunted a few times to each other, and made off in a leisurely manner, evidently in no fear. They were the first we had seen, and Hector was all excitement. He spoke rapidly to the two Bushmen who were with us, and then shouted some clicking, unintelligible gibberish after the retreating animals. At the call the whole troop halted, and their hoarse barks came back in reply. Again Hector shouted, and once again the baboons voiced a grunting mocking answer that John and I looked at each other in amazement! 'Look at Klaas!' he whispered.

"Klaas was a Hottentot who had been with the missionaries at Bethany, and spoke English. He spoke the Bushman 'click' too, but seldom had anything to do with the 'wild men,' as he called them. Now he stood listening to Hector's shouts to the baboons, and as he listened a look of the most abject terror came into his face, and he stood livid and trembling, staring in the direction of the beasts. Again Hector called; and then a shrill scream burst from the Hottentot's lips: 'No! no!' he shrieked. 'He is calling them back!' he gibbered, turning to us; 'they will tear us to pieces!!'

"The Bushmen were cowering in fear too; and still Hector, heedless of us all, called to the baboons; and their grunts came back in reply. And now the brutes were turning back towards us, and a thrill of fear came to me too, for there were at least a hundred of them, and a combined attack would have made short work of us, notwithstanding our Winchesters. I unslung mine; but John was before me a shot rang out, and the big leader flung up its long arms and fell dead. The troop halted, and then, before I could shoot, Hector sprang to where we knelt aiming and ordered us imperiously and passionately to stop. 'You fools!' he shrieked, 'you have spoiled all! How can I ever gain their confidence, how can I ever learn their speech and gain the proof of all that Darwin taught, if you murder them? Already from these Bushmen I have learnt much, and can make these wild men [he used the native expression quite naturally] understand, but much more is needed. Put up your guns: they shall come back!' Whilst we paused irresolute the baboons, picking up their fallen leader, made off across the mountain, in silence and with never a response to Hector's calls.

"From that time our leader's conduct became even stranger in fact he was as a man obsessed. He rarely spoke to us, but spent his whole time with the Bushmen, wandering away into the mountains and the thick jungle bordering the river, refusing our company, and no longer even carrying a rifle in a country at that time teeming with wild animals. His sole desire was to come into contact with the baboons, but for some days we saw nothing of them. He offered the Bushmen all sorts of rewards if they could capture and bring in a young one, but they had wild tales of raids by these strange beasts; of native women and children carried off by them, and becoming wild like their captors. At length, however, Hector's promises had effect: one evening the two Bushmen returned to camp dragging between them a half-grown baboon. It was surly, vicious, and so strong that they could scarce master it, but within twenty-four hours Hector had the animal subject to his will, and now the Bushmen were neglected for this strange new companion. That he could make himself understood to it was perfectly obvious; and they would wander away together, grunting and clicking all the time.

"The heat all this time was terrific, and the thought often came to me that possibly Hector had had a touch of sunstroke. Even his craze for finding a proof of Darwin's theory could, I thought, scarcely explain his half-mad conduct! He ate but little; his habits, once so precise, became careless and in fact almost brutal; and his brother's pained remonstrance with him only made matters worse. 'The Proof! the Proof!' he would answer us, fiercely and angrily; 'I am getting nearer to it every day. What matters what you think or care! But this one is too young. I must have an old one. He will tell me!' John and I had serious thoughts of taking him out of the wilderness by force; but whilst we hesitated the end came.

"One night, after a day of terrific heat, we were lying under a thorn tree on the hot sand, and hoping for the rain that had been threatening but would not fall. There was a moon; but its light was fitful, and the dark thunder-clouds occasionally obscured it. Away over the Tatas Berg Mountains the lightning was flickering, and John and I lay watching it, and wishing the storm would break for us too. Suddenly we heard the bark of a baboon from a peak near us. It was answered from the other side, and soon a harsh chorus resounded on either hand. We listened. They seemed to be narrowing in upon us. Klaas crept near us. 'Master,' he whispered in a frightened voice, 'they will kill us all or worse!' We looked at each other in the gloom. It might well be, and we had better be prepared. Without a word we rose and hurried to the tent, and there made ready our rifles. Then the same thought came simultaneously to us. Should we speak to Hector? He had of late used the smaller tent, a short distance away from our own his companion, the cursed baboon! We hurried towards it. It was empty. 'Hector! Hector!' John called out, softly at first, then loudly, frantically. But no answer came, except that now the mocking din of the baboons seemed to jeer at us. They appeared to be gathered near us, all together. As we ran towards the sound the moon burst through a rift in the clouds. There ahead of us, stark naked, and running swiftly towards the baboons, we saw the figure of Hector, his body gleaming white in the moonbeams, and by his side the grey figure of his baboon companion.

"We shouted, as over rocks and through scrub and thorns we ran and scrambled, gaining upon the fugitive. When he was but fifty yards ahead, he paused and turned, and the moonlight gleamed upon his gilded teeth as he laughed at us in maniac mockery. Then, even as we sprang towards him, a grey circle surged round him, and together they came towards us. For a time we were hard set to beat them off. When our Winchesters were empty a ring of dead lay around us, and then the moon was blotted out and dense darkness fell as the thunderstorm burst over us. Between the peals of thunder we could hear the hoarse barks of the main troop getting farther and farther away, but to follow was impossible. We expected to find the mangled body of Hector in the morning. Daylight showed no trace of him, however, and though we spent months searching the locality we never saw him again."

Jason stopped, and knocked his pipe out on his boot. I thought his tale was finished. "Horrible! horrible!" I said. "Little wonder you hate baboons! What became of his brother?"

"Wait!" said Jason, "that is only the first chapter of my story. John went back to England a morose, sad man. The incident had deeply affected me also, and we had become the closest of friends. Old Klaas came to Cape Town with us, and as we saw John waving to us from the fast receding mailboat the Hottentot said something I never forgot. 'Master,' he said, 'his brother I do not think he is dead! Something worse has happened to him: Klaas believes he is there in that strange place the Hottentots have all heard of there in the Tatas Berg, in the baboons' secret place.'

"Well, ten more, fifteen years passed, and I often heard from John. He had thrown up sport, and strangely enough had devoted himself entirely to the same scientific research that had been his brother's bane. Then his letters became fewer and fewer, and I heard nothing for many months when one day he walked into my room in Cape Town. He had just arrived from England, and after our first warm greeting he asked me eagerly if I were free to accompany him again to the scene of our awful experience. I was free enough, but reluctant. Why revive the horrors of that awful night! But he persuaded me, and a month later we were in the same region, and moreover had found old Klaas alive and hearty. John had become proficient in the Bushman and Hottentot tongues, as his brother had been; though where and how he had studied them I never knew. Would he, too, I wondered, try to obtain the Proof, as his poor mad brother had done? And when we first came in contact with the baboons I watched him closely. But he betrayed no madness only an intense interest in and hatred of them. Peculiarly enough, I thought at the time, although he shot the smaller ones mercilessly I never saw him shoot at the huge beasts we often saw watching us from the peaks. He must have noticed me watching him, for one day he turned and looked me full in the face, sadly and wistfully, as though reading my thoughts: 'No, no, Jason; never fear, old friend; I shall never seek the proof as Hector did. And yet, and yet, it is there!' I soon found that all his inquiries among the natives tended in one direction: he sought the whereabouts of the secret place of the baboons in which they all believed. But none could tell him, till one day in the wild and remote region between the Great Fish River and the Tatas Mountains we came upon Jantje, an old Hottentot, who told us that he had seen the place. He had been hunting for honey in the almost inaccessible mountains of that wild spot, and had one day found himself in a narrow gorge, looking down into what appeared to be a large crater. The sides were precipitous except at one spot where a narrow and tortuous canon made it possible to enter. And here, he assured us, was the stronghold of the baboons. Huge ones bigger than men, he told us and hundreds of them. And for a new gun and some powder and shot he would take us to the place. But he would not enter!

"Jantje got his gun; and three days later John, myself, and Klaas stood upon a mountain-top and looked into the spot he had described. It was at least five hundred feet deep, and perhaps a hundred yards across the bottom, which was flat and sandy. Even as we first looked into the place the baboons, several hundred strong, were surging through the gorge of which Jantje had spoken, away towards their feeding-ground by the Groot River. We watched them through our glasses. Many of them were of a man's size, and they were not like the ordinary baboon.

"John was all excitement. 'We will wait till they are clear away, and then we'll go down,' he said. I warned him that there were sure to be some left behind. But he was insistent. We were well armed, he urged, and he could see none. He badly wanted to see the place, and at last I consented. We each had a hundred rounds of ammunition, and if it came to a fight the three of us Klaas was also well armed could almost exterminate them. So, leaving the old man behind, we ventured down the narrow cleft clinging, scrambling, and occasionally using the rope. At length we stood in the open arena.

"At the bottom there was nothing living to be seen. A trickling stream issued from the rock on one side, and we drank before starting to explore the place. We found a piece of tattered clothing, and paused and looked at each other in dismay. There had been men there! But we discovered nothing else of importance as we continued our circuit of the crater. We had been engrossed in our investigations, however, and when we had finished it became clear that we had started our descent too late. The rapidly failing light showed us that the day was nearly at an end. The baboons might return at any time, and to fight them in the narrow ravine, without proper light, would be madness. Then came a warning shot fired by Jantje on the height above: the beasts were returning. To find some kind of hiding-place and lie there until the morrow was our only hope of safety. Luckily we discovered a sort of shallow cave that hid us well, with a huge boulder at the entrance that would if need be form a barrier. The cave might be the sleeping-place of one of the baboons; but it was our only chance, and we had barely taken possession before the advance guard of the baboons came hooting down the ravine and made for the drinking-place. Night was now falling fast, and it was dark before the main troop entered the crater. We could only dimly make out their forms, but their harsh barks were continuous. They did not come near us, and we sat and watched, and whispered to each other, and waited for the moon, which seemed long in coming. At last its bright light struck full into the crater, and we could see the baboons sitting together in a mass at the farther side. But not for long; for as we waited there was a movement among the animals, and two long files of them left the main body and came slowly towards the part in which we lay hidden. Tense with apprehension we sat and gazed, expecting that they would make a dash for us. They kept steadily on, however: two long lines of huge beasts a few yards apart, and between them a bigger one that walked almost erect. Within twenty yards of our cave they formed into a circle, the big one in the centre. He was as big as a man! Was he a man? But no, the clicking, grunting sound that issued from his throat was that of a baboon, though of a species different to the others. When the moonlight struck more fully on the shaggy head and face, they looked almost human! How the fangs glistened in the moonlight!

"The gestures of this strange animal became more excited, and the guttural speech if speech it was more passionate. I heard Klaas muttering he was praying. 'God have mercy!' I heard him say, 'they know we are here, they Oh! master, master, hold him, hold him!' But it was too late: John, with a wild scream of 'Hector! Hector!' sprang from the shelter of the cave, and, casting aside his rifle, ran straight at the strange figure in the middle of the circle. Had he gone mad? Who could save him now? Fast and furious Klaas's rifle and my own rang out, and in the dense group of animals the execution was so terrible that in a few minutes the bulk fled back to the farther end, and I ran to where John lay crushed in the arms of the baboon leader. The vile beast had its fangs fixed in his throat when I reached them. I fired a bullet through its head, and released my poor dead friend; and as the monster's shaggy head rolled back, and the moon's bright rays struck upon its glistening teeth, I saw with horror that they were of gold!"

5.   "BUSHMAN'S PARADISE"

Author's note: *The principal incident in the first part of this story, the shooting of the German soldier who found diamonds in German South-West Africa before they were heard of in Luderitzbucht, actually occurred, and the pocket-book containing the route to the oasis, now known as "Bush-man's Paradise," is still in existence. Names and localities have been altered, naturally, and the second part of the story is pure fiction.*

Jim Halloran was bored to death. With a natural curiosity he had drifted into Walfisch Bay, bitten as it were out of the huge expanse of German South-West Africa, vaguely expecting something out of the ordinary from such a queer locality. But he had found literally nothing to do. A few white officials and storekeepers, too slack even to be sick of their surroundings, and a few degraded families of Bushmen of uninteresting habits and extremely filthy, constituted the inhabitants. There was but little game in the small strip of British territory, and Halloran had made one or two abortive attempts to arrange a shooting and exploring trip into the German hinterland. Every one had warned him of the extreme peril from the shifting sand-dunes. Moreover, the war between the Germans and the Hereros was at its height, and the lieutenant in charge of the small garrison at Swakopmund had cautioned him not to venture beyond the limit of their patrols. There was no steamer for ten days, so that it was a veritable godsend to him when late one evening he received a message from the same friendly lieutenant to the effect that if he cared, he was welcome to accompany a patrol party which was to leave early the following morning in the direction of the little-known

Geiesib Mountains. He might bring his rifle, as there was a chance of some buck.

Daylight found Halloran in the saddle on his way to the German quarters. The patrol consisted of ten troopers in addition to his friend the lieutenant, who explained that two of his men who had been sent on patrol in that direction a few days previously had not returned, and that he hoped to find traces of them. "What do you think has happened to them?" Halloran asked. The German shrugged his shoulders. "A hundred things may have happened," he said "the Hereros or the Bushmen they may be under one of the shifting dunes or they are lost and may be dying of thirst who knows?"

The heat was terrific: the vibrant atmosphere over the red-hot sand looked as though it had become molten, and the glare to the eye was almost insufferable. There was not a breath of air stirring. Indeed, it was due solely to this fact that the patrol had ventured to cross the shifting dunes. Later, when the wind blew, it would be courting death to attempt it.

A few hours' sharp trot brought them to the nearest spurs of the mountain, where water had been found, by digging in the sand, bitter brak, but still drinkable, and here they had hoped to have found the lost troopers. But no trace of the missing men was to be seen. And over a hasty lunch Haussmann, the lieutenant, expressed his fear that they might never be found, but would go to swell the list of men who from time to time had disappeared from their little garrison. "In two years," he said, "I have lost nine men. First there were Schmidt, Muller, and Brandhof, who were lost in the colossal and never-to-be- forgotten storm soon after I arrived; then my orderly Goertz went, and with him another. Then Kramer yes but Kramer, that was different!"

Halloran was curious. "What happened to Kramer?" he asked. And the German told him a strange story. Kramer was a queer mountebank sort of a chap who before conscription claimed him had been clown in a circus, and his antics and gymnastic feats had made him very popular with his fellow-troopers. He had been a good soldier too; and when he had become separated from his fellow-trooper in a sandstorm a day or more south of Swakopmund, and his companion had struggled through without him, no effort had been spared in searching for the missing man. But to no purpose; months passed and he had been almost forgotten. And then, to every one's surprise, he had one day turned up, safe and sound, at the camp. He was nearly naked, and bore traces of having lived like a savage, and the lieutenant believed that he had become affected by his privations and was slightly mad. At any rate, he had told a strange and improbable story. Lost in the drifting sands, he had struggled on he knew not whither until his horse dropped, then on foot, and, with all sense of direction utterly lost, he had staggered on till tired nature gave out and he sank to the ground in a dead faint. The storm must have abated shortly after, for he woke to find himself nearly buried but with the air clearer, and, somewhat refreshed, he had again moved on, until, water gone and nearly dead, he had eventually staggered clear of the sands and right into the arms of a number of Bushmen. For some reason they had spared his life. Later his acrobatic feats had made him even popular with them. His story went on to tell of a well-wooded oasis where the Bushmen lived, with water and game in plenty.

"All this is probably true," said the lieutenant, "but his brain must have been somewhat turned, for he declared that in this oasis the Bushmen's children made playthings of big rough diamonds the size of walnuts!" Kramer had watched for an opportunity to escape, but when it came he had had no chance of bringing away any of the stones, as the Bushmen had a vague idea that the white men valued them highly and that if they knew of their presence in the oasis their refuge would soon be lost to them. "He stuck to his tale," said the lieutenant, "and his great idea was that I should help him to go back with a strong expedition as soon as his time of service expired, and he would make me a rich man. Of course," he continued dogmatically, "there are no diamonds in this country, worse luck! so Kramer was laughed at by everybody." He became madder than ever, sullen and morose. He thought of nothing but his mad dream of diamonds. A few months previously his discharge had come, and within a few days he had again disappeared into the un-known. He had bought a mule, and had gone away laden with water-bags, laughed and jeered at by his late comrades. He had never been heard of in the interval. "But," said the lieutenant abruptly, "we must be off, as we must go on at least two or three hours further east, and I should suggest, Mr. Halloran, that if you care to do so you could stay here till our return. You are likely to get a shot here by the water."

Halloran agreed, and the patrol trotted away over the thick sand that skirted the mountains eastward. The tale told by Haussmann had a strange fascination for him. Himself something of a prospector, the story of the diamonds did not appear so wild and improbable to him as it did to the matter-of-fact Teuton. He had often wished for a chance to pros-pect the slopes of these very mountains, which looked very promising for gold but diamonds! Was it possible? Choosing a spot among the rocks where he was somewhat sheltered from the sun and could command a view of the little pool and its approaches, he sat down to muse over the story and to await the chance of a possible shot. A couple of hours passed. The stillness and intense heat combined to make him drowsy, and he woke with a start to find he had been dreaming of diamonds as big as tennis balls. "Bad sportsman," he yawned. "I shall never get a shot this way," and, rubbing his eyes, he peered cautiously round in search of game. Not a thing in sight in any direction. Stop! was that a speck moving on a distant spur of the mountain? The atmosphere was deceptive, but surely it was some animal approaching in his direction. He had up till then forgotten his binoculars, but he was now wide awake and, looking first to his rifle, he got out his glasses and twisted them into focus upon the moving object in the distance. A startled exclamation rose to his lips as the field-glasses covered the moving spot; it was a man. Yes running, stumbling, crouching and at times almost crawling the object which he saw was a white man, naked except for a few rags. His desperate haste and the glances he threw back continually showed that he was being pursued. Even as Halloran gazed, figure after figure came running into view over the slope behind the forlorn and desperate-looking fugitive blacks these, and by their diminutive size he knew them for Bushmen. There were seven or eight of them in sight. How many more were behind he could not of course guess, nor did he stop to look, for every manly instinct in his body sent him flying out of his shelter towards the hunted man. He must shoot quick, for it was plain the Bushmen were gaining on their quarry. So, shouting with all his might, Halloran ran forward. A couple of hundred yards' sprint and they were within range. Down he went on one knee, and crack, crack went the sporting Mauser. The vibration of the hot air was sufficient excuse for bad shooting, and it was not until he had emptied his magazine that he had the satisfaction of sending the leading Bushman sprawling. But the others did not pause, and as Halloran thrust another clip into the magazine and ran forward again, shouting and using some very bad language in his excitement, he saw the leading figure throw up his hands and fall forward upon his face. He had the range better now, and was getting near. A second and a third Bushman fell dead, but the others made no attempt to retreat, and appeared to be rifling the body in frantic haste. Again Halloran paused, and sent a bullet into the bunch. Now they were flying away, leaving four of their number behind them. Shot after shot was sent after them till they were out of range, beyond the ridge, by which time Halloran had reached the fallen white man. There he lay, stone dead, with a Bushman's poisoned arrow between his shoulders and his body already swollen and horrible from the deadly poison. A white man without doubt, his feet bare and bleeding from his awful flight, his few poor rags almost torn from his body by the Bushmen. Though tanned almost black he had been a fair man, and his blue eyes stared horribly. He was beyond all succour, whoever he was, and

Halloran turned savagely to the remnants of the murderous band. They had paid dearly. Three were stone dead. A fourth lay dying where Halloran had brought him down in his flight, and near him lay a tattered pocketbook. Halloran picked this up. He knew what name he should find in it before he glanced at the contents. Yes, there was the name: "Heinrich Kramer." It was the man who had gone back for the diamonds. This, then, was why the Bushmen had followed and killed him and rifled the body. Halloran searched also, but the natives had done their work well. Nothing was to be found. However, as he turned to look at the wounded Bushman, who was in his death-agony, there fell from the stunted black fingers a pure and flawless diamond, lustrous and dazzling in the burning sunshine, and so perfect that it might just have left the hands of the cutter. . . . So it was true, after all!

Half an hour later the patrol came back at a gallop, having heard the continuous firing. A few words explained all. It was Kramer right enough. As it was useless following the Bushmen, poor Kramer was buried and the patrol returned to Swakopmund, having found no trace of the men for whom they had been searching. In the presence of the men Halloran had not mentioned the pocketbook or diamond, but that night he told Haussmann all. The pocket-book contained many details, and although much was in cypher, the route taken by Kramer in reaching the oasis the second time was clearly noted. And between them a plan was formed.

Six months later Halloran arrived in Cape Town, having spent the interim in Europe, where he had made certain arrangements. He was met by his friend (and partner in the venture) the lieutenant on three months' sick leave and between them the expedition was organised which was to make both their fortunes. From Europe, Halloran had shipped half a dozen camels, and these ungainly beasts, in charge of two Arab drivers, formed an important item in his scheme. A small tug was chartered for three months, and a week after sailing from Cape Town the party landed on a wild and desolate part of the coast a hundred and fifty miles south of Walfisch Bay. The reason for choosing this spot was that, according to the directions in the pocket-book, it appeared clear that by striking inland due east from thereabouts they would reach the oasis much quicker than by the actual route followed by Kramer. But they knew it to be a waterless waste for at least four days' journey how much more it was impossible to say hence the camels, and hence also the numerous small barrels of water which formed an equally important part of the tug's cargo. There were four white men in the party Halloran, his younger brother Frank, Haussmann the German lieutenant, and a friend of the latter named Haupt. From Swakopmund, Haussmann had brought two Hottentots who could speak the extraordinary Bushman "click" language. These, with the Arab camel-men, made the actual number up to eight. Each was well armed, for Halloran, though he hoped to get the diamonds without violence, had a notion that in an extreme case a good deal could be done by eight determined men armed with Mausers and with plenty of ammunition. The tug with its crew of six men was to remain anchored in the little cove, keeping a sharp look-out shorewards. Halloran had chosen his time well. The windy season was at an end and there was no great probability of the much- dreaded sandstorms arising. The moon was nearly at its full and they would thus be able to keep a sharp look-out at night, and travel if they wished to. Five of the camels were laden with water casks, which were to be buried at intervals along the route, accurate bearings of each spot to be taken, and thus a safe line of retreat would be provided should such prove necessary. Speed was unnecessary on the outward journey, and the party walked, the sixth camel carrying their stores, ammunition, and a large assortment of Manchester trading goods likely to appeal to the aesthetic taste of the Bushmen. And so one evening as the last flaming rays of the setting sun were being vanquished by the soft moonlight, the venturesome party waved farewell to the watchers on the little tug and started on their journey over the seemingly illimitable sand-dunes. They trekked in single file and by the aid of the stars and a compass easily kept their eastward course. The murmur of the surf grew fainter and fainter until not a sound broke the stillness, the soft footfall of the camels being inaudible even to the men who led them. Halloran had enjoined silence for some reason, and he stopped his brother irritably when that usually irrepressible youth started to whistle feebly. With an occasional rest the expedition made slow but certain headway during the night, halting for the day when the rapidly brightening east warned them that old Sol would soon have to be reckoned with. A barrel of water was buried in the sand, a bamboo brought for the purpose being planted upright near the spot, and after a hasty breakfast the tired men were soon asleep under a light awning carried for the purpose; one man, however, being constantly on watch. By noon the heat had become intolerable. Roasting in the sun seemed preferable to stewing under the canvas, and by three o'clock the party were on their way again. They rested at midnight, and rested better. The fourth night found them still on the sand-dunes, and by this time the weird journey was beginning to tell upon the white men. The silence and mystery of the night, the vast expanse of sand shown so vaguely in the moonlight, the soft-treading, grotesquely-shaped camels, which seemed far less real and tangible than the black shadows thrown by them across the sand, and by day the blinding glare of the sun thrown back from the all-surrounding sand so fiercely that in spite of their sun-goggles they were nearly blinded, combined to make them high- strung and irritable. On the fourth night it fell to young Frank Halloran to take first watch. He had grumbled at it as unnecessary, for so far they had seen no living creature not even a bird. But though he grumbled he kept a sharp look-out, for he was conscious of a queer uneasy feeling that someone or something was watching him in turn. The moon was bright, but a slight haze seemed to hang over the sand, making objects a short distance away look vague and indistinct. He could see nothing, peer as he would into the soft, dim distance, but he could not shake off the uneasy feeling. Time wore on, half his watch was over. What was that? Surely something moving? His rifle came to his shoulder, the report rang out, and his comrades were awake instantly. Nothing could be found. His brother rated him for shooting at what was probably a jackal, if, indeed, it had not been pure imagination. But daylight, though it showed nothing to the white men, showed something to the wonderfully trained eyes of the Hottentots. "Bushman!" said Gert, the elder of the two. The spoor came from the east and led back in the same direction. Halloran was quite elated. He took it for proof that they were on the right track. . . .

All this can be gathered from the notes in Halloran's handwriting, which are to be found in the pocket-book that had belonged to Kramer. The book had had a strange fascination for him, and he had used it for his own diary. Indeed, these short and sometimes disconnected sentences are the only real record of the grim tragedy that followed.

The little caravan got through the sand-belt safely in six days, and without further alarms from the Bushmen. Then came stony kopjes with stunted bush, and here and there traces of game and lions. Water could not be far off. On the tenth day they had found the oasis, and by sending the Hottentots on ahead with presents they had met with no open hostility from the Bushmen. There was plenty of water. Halloran seems to have tried to get the diamonds by bartering goods for them, but for some days the Bushmen had kept up the pretence that there were no diamonds there. Then force was threatened and a demonstration made as to what could be done with eight repeating rifles. Finally Halloran seems to have laid violent hands on the chief and to have held him to ransom against the production of the stones. But from this time the pocket-book speaks best for itself.

"August 13th. They have given in. Gert has taken the chief's message, and they have brought us a skin-bag full of the stones. These are diamonds right enough fine big stones of eight or nine carats, nearly all the same size and we are rich men. The sight of them made us greedy, and we told the chief they were not enough. He told us through Gert that we had broken our word. Have we? Of course we did not tell him for how many diamonds we would let him go. Besides, we will give him all the trading goods in return. He said something to his wives which even the Hottentots could not understand, but they came again with a dozen very large diamonds, and we let him go.

"I do not like the look of things. Every Bushman has disappeared. Do they intend to attack us later? We shall water the camels as soon as it is cool enough, fill our water-bags and start on our return journey. Luckily we have buried water all the way back, we can travel lightly and rapidly.

"What shall we do? They have poisoned the water-pools. One of the Arabs, the younger Hottentot, and three of our camels are dead. Lucidly, the poison was swift, and they fell dead before Gert and the other camels could get to the pool. We must fly as best we may, our nearest cask is only twelve hours away.

"14th. We are resting the camels for a short spell about three hours from the first cask. We have neglected the camels in our anxiety for the diamonds. They have had no water for three days. We must give them most of the first cask. It is awful work riding two on a camel, but we can get through in four or five days, and then---

"I am almost too stunned to write. We found the cask. We had not thought of its being tampered with. My poor brother Frank drank the first pannikin greedily, and fell dying at our feet as he drank. The fiends had found the water and poisoned it. As the poor boy lay dying in my arms the water ran unheeded into the sands. A camel sucked it up eagerly. It is dead also. We must on again. Surely they cannot have found the other casks.

"17th. I am alone. The others are all dead all. We tried the water in the other casks by giving some first to the camels. It had all been poisoned. They are following us too, but too far off to shoot them. Gert went mad and drank the water it was so bright and clear. Each time we hoped they might not have found the next cask; but so far they have found them all. There are three more. The young German turned back to die fighting the black devils. We heard him shooting for a long time, but he must be dead too. The Arab was missing in the night. He too had gone back. . . . We have dragged on till within eighteen hours of the coast, but I can go no further. When the lieutenant and I dug up the last cask we cast lots as to who should try it. It fell to him. I wished him to sip it only, but once his lips were wet I could not tear him away. . . . He cursed me as he died. ... I have all the diamonds now and would give them all for a drink of pure water. . . . Surely they cannot have found the other casks. I will win through yet. It is but six hours to the next cask.

"Another cask but I dare not. It is bright and cool and clear; but so were the others! And yet I am dying of thirst. I can go no further. . . . They are creeping nearer. They know my rifle has gone, and I know that if I do not drink they will shoot me as they did that other man through the back with a poisoned arrow. But I will not wait for that. This water looks so cool and clear, surely . . ."

The diary ends abruptly, A week later the engineer and skipper of the little tug, venturing across the sands in the hope of meeting the party returning, found Halloran's body by the side of the water-cask. Near by lay the fatal pocket-book. But the diamonds had gone.

6.   "THE DRINK OF THE DEAD"

A LEGEND OF BUSHMANLAND

This tale was told me over a camp-fire in lonely Bushmanland.

A wild and desolate land it is, but little known except to the occasional nomad "trek-boer," who in the seasons when rain has made it possible wanders from water-hole to water-hole with his scanty flocks and herds; or to the mounted trooper on his long and lonely patrol; or the even more infrequent prospector in his search for the mineral wealth that abounds in the district, but which scarcity of water and cost of transport have so far rendered useless. A land with a character all its own of wide stretches of low grey bush, intermingled with the vivid-green patches of luxuriant "melkbosch," giving deceptive promise of non-existent moisture; of level plains, gay with brilliant flowers, from which long humped ranges of granite rise in serried lines.

A common necessity had drawn two of us white men to a distant and isolated water-hole, which to our dismay we had found dry and empty. Neither of us knew of other water within twelve hours' trek, our beasts were tired, and it was a great relief when Karelse, my Hottentot driver, declared he knew of good water only about four hours away. I wondered I had never heard of it before, but Karelse, who knew every inch of the country, was confident that though he had never been to the spot we should find plenty of water there; and, sure enough, nightfall brought us to the place, and there was water in abundance. Here we shared coffee and biltong, and afterwards sat smoking and yarning by the cheerful blaze of the dry fire-bush.

The night was wild and stormy, and a cold wind blew in sharp gusts round the fantastic pile of rocks that rose abruptly from the small deep pool of black-looking water, sending the sparks swirling upwards and causing the flames to leap fiercely, whilst the flicker of the fire shone on the glittering "baviaan-spel" of the rocks, and the black shadows danced to the whistle of the wind.

Overhead the sky seemed charged with rain the heavy, hurrying clouds lowered and trailed and seemed as though at any moment they might launch a deluge upon the parched and yearning veldt; but the promise was ever an empty one, for not a drop fell, and the rain-charged phalanxes sped onward and ever onward, to shed their precious burthen upon distant and more-favored fields. . . .

Jason I had met before. Like myself he was a prospector, and had known many lands. He was a reserved, reliable man, who possessed a habit of silence rare amongst men of our fraternity. Our talk had been of Brazil, where we had both spent many years of our youth, and almost unconsciously we had fallen into Portuguese a language we both spoke fluently.

It was then that the Other Man appeared. Suddenly, silently, and alone he stepped from among the flickering shadows of the rocks, so abruptly as to cause both Jason and I to start up with an exclamation. By the uncertain light of the fire he appeared to be an elderly man of medium size, swarthy, weather-beaten, and bearded to the eyes. He strode to the fire, extended a limp, cold hand to Jason and I in turn with an almost inaudible greeting, and crouched down by the dying blaze, his dark eyes bent upon the glowing embers. Naturally expecting him to be Dutch, both Jason and I had greeted him in the usual manner by giving our own names in self-introduction. He had made no reply; but though our hearth was but a campfire in a wild country, we felt that whoever he was he was in a measure our guest, and therefore we made no immediate attempt to find out who or what he was. Still he did not speak. He put aside our proffered coffee, gently but without a word, and sat glowering and gazing into the fire.

At last Jason spoke to him direct first in Dutch, and, getting no reply, in English.

"Come far?" he queried.

There was no sign that the man had heard. Jason looked at me with a lift of the eyebrow. Then I tried.

"Farming?" I asked.

No answer.

"Trading?"

Still no answer.

"Man's dumb!" grunted Jason.

But he was muttering now. Gradually his words became clearer, and to our amazement he was speaking Portuguese!

"Pesquisadores pesquisadores," he murmured, "como nos outras dos tempos antigos." (Prospectors searchers for wealth, like we others of the olden days.) "... Searching for that which is not yours, but mine, mine by every right. . . . But you will never find it or if you do your bones will lie beside those others beneath the black water, where the dead drink . . .!"

His mutterings became again inarticulate. I looked at Jason. He sat staring open-mouthed at our strange visitor. For my own part I confess I was puzzled and somewhat startled. Jason's eyes left the stranger abruptly, and met my own, and mutually and silently our lips framed the word "Mad!" Yes, surely he must be mad, this strange man who spoke of the "ancient days" in a tongue rarely heard in this part of Africa; but what was he doing here, here, alone, in this desolate spot, full fifty miles from human habitation.

And as we looked at each other in doubt and hesitation the stranger began again to speak, first in broken, disconnected sentences. But gradually the strange, far-away tone like that of a man talking in his sleep became clearer and more connected, and soon Jason and I were gazing at him as though spellbound, and drinking in every word of the queer archaic-sounding Portuguese in which he told his weird story fragment, delirium, wanderings of a madman, call it what you will.

"... There were Bushmen, then wild dwarf men who shot with poisoned arrows, and had seen no white man before . . . .

"Alvaro Nunes had still five charges for his arquebus, and I as many for my hand petronel. . . . When they heard the thunder of the powder they cast aside their weapons and crawled to us on their knees, taking us for gods. . . . And bearing in mind all that the shipwrecked Castilian we had found at Cabo Tormentoso had told us of the mine of precious stones, we hastened to propitiate them in every way. . . . The gauds we had brought, gay beads, bright kerchiefs, and the like with these we won our way to their goodwill. They hunted for us; of buck and of wild game they brought us abundance; but though months passed we were no nearer that which we sought the mine of bright stones such as the Spanisher had shown us and the whereabouts of which these strange black, dwarfish people alone knew. Never could we master their strange tongue like to the creaking and rustling of dry bones upon a gibbet more than the speech of humans and time and patience alone showed us a way. Their man of magic held great power over them. He was of another race, of our own stature, and with a yellow skin. He had another tongue than these dwarf men of the bush, and this Alvaro and I learnt when his suspicion of us gave way and he found that we wished not to alienate the tribe from his authority. . . . For the Spanisher had said: 'Their magician, because of his black magic, he alone hath the secret of the mine of stones like unto those of Golconda.' . . . Little did we fear his magic we who feared nothing in heaven or earth or in the waters beneath Alvaro and I, old freebooters of the Spanish Main; but they others Luiz Fonseca, Jose Albuquerque, and Antonio Mendez brave men, but ignorant ship-men, they were fearful of the witch-doctor and his black art.

"Then when N'buqu, the witch, had heard all of the wonders of our land across the great water, he would fain plot to come with us and see all these wondrous things of which we spake. And cunningly Alvaro led him on day by day until he was all impatient to leave this tribe of dwarfs, who were not even his own kinsmen. Then when all was ripe he told him that with us there were no wild lands full of buck for those who cared to shoot them, that our wealth was in red gold and shining stones! And at long last he showed the stone taken from the Spanisher at the Cape of Storms. . . .

"At night when the moon was full N'buqu took us to the black water-pit lying deep and dark at the foot of the rocky hill. Ten fathoms deep was it and full to the brim with icy water. Many times had we drank from it, for though all around the land lay parched in the torrid heat the black water-pit was always full to the brim. . . .

"But what magic was this? Here was no water, but a yawning shaft gaped black and dismal where the pool had been. The shipmen shrank back in dismay. 'Here is magic!' they muttered fearfully, crossing them-selves. N'buqu laughed. He also had learnt something of our tongue, and understood. 'No magic is here,' said he, "tis but a spring from yonder hill that fills this pool, and it needs but to turn the stream aside and the water will all drain away. Later I will show!'

"From a fire-stick he had brought he lit a torch of dry wood. By its glare we saw that a hide ladder dangled from an overhanging rock into the deep pit. Down it N'buqu led the way, followed by us all in turn the shipmen with many muttered prayers and misgivings. . . . Slimy and dank was the fearsome place, but the bottom was firm and rocky, and from it there branched a cavern wide enough for us all to walk abreast. Gently it led upward . . . and then we stood in a broader cavern, where the light from the torch in every direction flashed back from a myriad dazzling points: ceiling, walls, every rock protuberance, even the very floor gleamed and scintillated till the whole place blazed as though on fire. N'buqu thrust the torch into Alvaro's hand. 'Look!' he cried, and smote with a spear he carried at the wall of the cavern. At the light blow a handful of the flashing points fell to the floor. We picked them up. They were the 'bright stones' of the Spanisher they were diamonds! Here was wealth beyond conception wealth beside which the fabled Golconda would be as nought, wealth untold for us all. But on the floor among the flashing gems there lay many white bones the bones of dead men. . . . Wealth, vast wealth for us all, and yet we quarreled there as to the division of the stones, and as to how we were to get them away. 'Get all we can at once and flee this very night!' urged the shipmen. 'And die of thirst in the desert places!' said Alvaro for it was the season of drought! 'Stay only until we can fill our water- skins,' they counseled. But Alvaro and myself we were wiser.

"N'buqu his must be the plan. He knew the best paths back to the Cape of Tempests, he knew the water-holes; we must be guided by his counsel. And we forced them to listen. Yes, he had a plan. Three nights hence we must flee. He would have water ready in skins. Meanwhile each night he would divert the water, and we must descend and collect the stones so that we should have enough for all. At night the tribe believed that the spirits of the dead came to the black water to drink, and always avoided the spot. . . . And by the light of the flickering torch we broke down showers of the glittering stones from the soft blue rock in which they were embedded till our pouches were full and the torch had burned out. Then we stumbled and groped our way over slime and bones till we came to the shaft, and one by one we climbed up and out into the fair white moonlight. . . .

"Fools! fools! The shipmen quarreled over the stones the first day. Alvaro lent them dice and they gambled with each other for their new-found wealth. And as Alvaro wished, they quarreled; and Albuquerque and Fonseca drew steel upon each other, and there in the sunshine stabbed each other to death. 'The more for us,' said Alvaro, and we divided the stones they fought for.

"That night we four went again to the black water. Once more we loaded our pouches and climbed out one by one. I the first, for I was faint with the air of the cavern. Then came N'buqu. But Alvaro came not, nor Mendez the shipman. Impatiently I shook the ladder: it was near dawn. Then at length came Alvaro. He was ghastly in the moonlight. And at the top he began to pull up the ladder he had climbed by. 'But Mendez?' I muttered. He answered not, but still hauled the hide rope. Then I seized him by the shoulder and looked in his face. There was blood upon him. 'He struck me from behind,' he said; 'my vest of mail saved me; he is dead. The more for us!' I liked not Alvaro's face, and looked to my dagger lest to-morrow he should say 'The more for me.' . . .

"That third night Alvaro and I for the last time descended the black shaft. Well watched we each the other. He had both dagger and arquebus, and I my hand petronel and dagger too. N'buqu came not down with us, feigning that he must prepare all things that we might flee as soon as we had loaded our pouches for the last time. . . . There he left us in the black shaft my life-long comrade and I; and by reason of the lust of wealth that came upon me and because of the fear of that which I saw in Alvaro's eye I struck him unawares as he knelt for the last gem. Deep behind the neck my dagger drank his blood. His vest of mail did not save him from me! ... And turning to flee hastily with all the stones, I found the ladder drawn up and N'buqu laughing at me from above. "'Ho! ho! white man, white wizard!' he called. 'Ye who would show me the wondrous things of thine own land. How fares it with ye now? Surely thou hast enough of the bright stones now thy dead comrade's share and all he had taken; thou hast them all! Handle them, gaze on them, eat of them, drink of them; for of a surety naught else will there be for thee to eat and drink! Ho! ho! surely the black man's magic is vain against the wisdom of the white!'

"And thus he taunted me, whilst vainly I strove by means of my dagger to cut footholds in the slimy walls of the shaft and thus climb to freedom. But the holes crumbled as soon as my weight bore on them, and after falling again and again I desisted in despair. . . . And ever the yellow fiend above taunted me, and it was abundantly clear that he had but feigned to fall in with our scheme the more fully to encompass our destruction. . . . Dawn found me raving in terror of my coming fate alone with the bodies of the friend whom I had slain and the shipman who had been by him slain. Terror had helped to parch my tongue with thirst, and both shaft and cavern, though moist, were drained too dry to afford one mouthful of the precious fluid. Yet though longing for water I knew well that when N'buqu should choose again to direct the stream I should drown like any rat. The day passed. I heard the frightened mutterings of the dwarf men as they crowded round the mouth of the shaft seeking the black water that had vanished; but at my first hoarse shout they fled, yelling in alarm. Day turned to night, and I had become as one dead. The ghosts of dead Alvaro and Mendez and a thousand others crowded round me, gibing, and mouthing, and seeking too for the black water. Again day, and again night came and went. Still the water I longed for and yet feared came not. I suffered the tortures of the damned, and fain would I have scattered my throbbing brains with that last charge of my hand petronel; but ever as I raised it dead Alvaro caught my hand in an icy grip and I could not die. . . .

"Then again I heard N'buqu, and with him certain men of the dwarfs he ruled. And in their whistling, creaking tongue I heard him hold forth: 'Lo! ye who doubted me, thus do I show my power. These other white gods that came from afar, ye thought them stronger than I, yet have I caused their utter destruction. But because of the little faith ye had in me, and as a sign of my power and displeasure, have I also caused the spirits that dwell in the black pool to take away the water that is life to ye all!'

"Then I heard them moaning and begging for the water, and the voice of the witch-doctor ordering them to lie flat on their faces and look not up whilst he forced the spirits to bring back that which they had taken. Then he called to me in my own tongue loudly: 'Ho! thou white god! eat thou thy fill of the bright stones; of water thou shalt soon drink plenty!' And I knew that he would soon move that rock whereby the water could be diverted back to the pit. But even as he gibed at me, leaning over the brink, dead Alvaro's ice-cold hand guided my petronel till it covered the black fiend's body, and the iron ball struck full and true below his throat. Down at my feet hurtled the body, and at the report I could hear the dwarfs shriek and fly away from the spot in fear.

"Not dead, but dying was he, for his magic was naught against the weapons of the white man. Yet magic had he, and as he died so did he curse me and cast over me a spell of terror: 'Thou shalt guard well thy bright stones, oh, slayer of thy friend!' he shrieked. 'Water shalt thou have, and yet shall never quench thine awful thirst; hunger shall consume thee and thou shalt not eat; thou shalt long for death, yet shalt thou not die!' And cursing thus he died; and his ghost joined the band of weird watchers in the cavern of bright stones. . . .

"And the tribe of dwarfs one by one died of thirst, for it was a year of fearful heat, and they knew of no other water. Day by day they came shrieking and praying to the spirits of the black shaft to give them back the water. Day by day they flung living men into the pit as sacrifice to join the spirits below, till all, all were dead. Yet could I not die! . . .

"Over their bleached bones the black water again runs. Below, guarded by the dread watchers, lie the bright stones. Seek not the spot, ye white men who speak the old tongue, lest ye too watch for ever; for the place is accursed! . . ."

The strange narration ended as it began, not abruptly, but in indistinct mutterings.

Half fascinated, Jason and I had followed every word of the strange archaic Portuguese. The rhythmic sentences seemed to have had an almost hypnotic effect upon us, for neither of us afterwards remembered how and when we fell asleep.

I was awakened by Karelse shaking me. It was just break of day. I felt heavy, sleepy, and confused, and for a moment remembered nothing.

"Coffee, baas," said the Hottentot; and as I sipped it I remembered. I looked round. Jason was sleeping like a log. Our strange visitor had gone. "Where is the other baas?" I inquired of Karelse. He stared at me, and then looked over at Jason. "No, no," I said impatiently, "the old baas that came in the night?" Karelse's face was a study. He had evidently seen no one, though the boy's fire had been not twenty yards from our own. Had I dreamt the whole thing? I strode over and roused Jason. He woke with a startled exclamation. His first words assured me the old man had been there. "Damn that mad chap," he said. "His horrible old yarn made me dream badly. Where is he?" Karelse stared from one to the other, his yellow face a queer ashen grey. He was plainly frightened. "Come," said I to Jason, "let us go and have a sluice: there is water in plenty." I led the way to the pool. It had been too dark for us to see it properly when we had arrived the evening before. We bent over the dark, clear water. Sheer and black the pit went down, and it was plainly of great depth. And from the brink the granite kopje rose abruptly. Jason and I looked at each other, then at Karelse.

"Karelse," I asked, "have you ever been here before?"

"No, baas," he faltered; "there is always plenty of good water here, they say, but the place has a bad name and no one comes here. They say it is haunted."

"What do they call the place?" I asked.

"Dood Drenk," he said "the Drink of the Dead!"

7. THE WATERS OF ERONGO

North-East of Swakopmund, and somewhere where the line that runs the copper ore down from Otari has a station called Omaruru, there stands a mass of huge table-topped mountains. At the time of which I write they were known as the Erongos, so named after a famous chief of the Gainin Bushmen, who had made something of a stand there against the invading Damaras that eventually "ate up" both him and his tribe.

Even in that land, where most mountains are table-topped, and where the flat plateau above and the plain beneath represent geological epochs that are divided by aeons of years, these Erongo Mountains are remarkable; for they have never been climbed. From their base thick vegetation can be seen crowning the inaccessible summit, and in several places water flows in gushing cataracts down the steep cliffs that frown upon the plain on every side.

This mountain had always had a great fascination for me; and once or twice, in the old days, before the railway came, and when we used to water our transport animals at these same streams, I attempted to climb its steep sides, full of curiosity to see what the top might be like.

But I never got within a thousand feet of it, for the crowning bastions are almost sheer, and would need a better cragsman than myself to negotiate.

Isolated, and rising straight from the plain to a height of about 3,000 feet, it formed a prominent landmark for those few traders or prospectors who, in the old days, returned from their trips to the north to Walfisch Bay by this route; and I was glad indeed to see its huge bulk towering up one day more years ago than I care to remember when trekking in from a

long expedition in the Kaokoveld for it meant that my long journey was
nearly finished.

With my wagon I had as cook and roust-about an old Englishman
named Jim Blake, who had ran away from his ship at Walfisch Bay
many years before, and who had traversed the country in all directions,
since then, as few men had. In spite of the many years he had spent
there, and the fact that he spoke many of the native dialects well, his
Cockney accent was as pronounced as ever it could have been when he
first shipped at Limehouse; and he had, apparently, a wholesale con-
tempt for everything, and everybody, but himself.

As his employer, he tolerated me, and as he was invaluable in many
ways, I tolerated him in return, but he had one habit that always annoyed me immensely. In season and out of season he would say: "Yer
don't know heverythink if yer thinks yer does!"; and I could never break
him of it.

Well, the evening that I speak of, we outspanned under the cliffs of
Erongo, and the oxen drank deep.

We had had a very successful trip, and I felt at peace with all mankind, as I sat smoking, and watching the setting sun turn the tall rocks
from gold to crimson, and thence through a whole gamut of purples,
violets and mauves to the cold grey of twilight.

"Pritty, 'aint it?" said a voice at my elbow. It was old Blake. His maho-
gany face shone with the effects of the first soap and water he had been
able to use for weeks, for we had been very short of water; and even his
arms showed the tattoo-marks that were usually hidden by the grime
inseparable to life in the desert.

"Yes," I answered, "it's beautiful, the most beautiful mountain I know
in Africa. I wonder what's on top? I've had a go at climbing it myself
several times but, of course, it can't be done. The Bushmen couldn't,
Erongo himself only had his werf half-way up when he fought the Damaras. No one has ever climbed it!"

"You don't know heverythink if yer thinks yer does," sniffed old Jim;
"you're wrong. I've bin up it meself!"

"Rubbish, Jim!" I said; "don't talk rot. How far have you been up, anyway? As far as the bottom of the big fall, I suppose?"

"To the top and all over it," said old Jim. "Oh, I knows yer don't believe. But it's gospel. You don't know heverythink!"

"No, that's true, Jim," said I meekly, for I wanted his yarn. "I know
you sailormen can climb better than I ever shall but how did you do it?
Ropes? Ladders? . . . How?"

"No," he answered slowly, turning his quid in his cheek, and spitting
with great precision at a blue-headed lizard that had emerged from a

crack in the rock and sat eyeing us. "Got yer!" he went on as the small reptile retired in considerable discomfiture.

"No, neether ladders nor ropes. If yer reely wants ter know, I were carried up!"

"Oh, you can chuckle, but so it were! Twenty year or more agone I came here fust. There was four of us white men; me as cook, two prospectors, and the perfesser.

"He was a queer bloke, that perfesser, clever, too, but bless yer he didn't know heverythink! I'd bin with him a long time, and he used ter tell me more'n he tole the other fellers . . . a clever sort of chap . . . but he didn't know heverythink. And he 'ad one great pecooliarity: he was everlastingly afeard of getting old! He must ha' bin well over fifty, but he used ter get himself up outrageous young: and when I docked his shavingwater he cussed most wonderful!

"'Cleanliness, and stric' observance of rules of life that is the only way ter keep young, Blake,' he would say ter me.

"Well, in them days, bein' young, I didn't see much in what he said, and if I got a wash once a month I was werry well satisfied; and arter a while this 'ere washing business of his got on my nerves. 'Cause, as yer know, when water's been used fer a bath, yer can't werry well use it fer anything but washing up, or biling pertaters, or sich like, and he was the wastefullest man I ever had to cook for. Well, we comes up here on our way to the Koaka Velt on some kind of scientific trip er other I dunno, and it didn't matter as long as I was paid and the two prospectors they brings in gold, and tin, and copper, and all sorts of muck, and the perfesser was busy 'blow-piping' and 'classifying' and what not, and every day he gets more 'centrick. Then he gets sick only a bit of fever, but it laid him out bad for a time: and he couldn't shave, and he couldn't bath, and that hurt him wuss'n the fever. We was here, then; jist in this same camp. And when he got well enough to talk again I took him his cawfee one morning, and sees him a-looking at himself in a little glass: and he looked fair frightened! He'd got a week's bristles on, and they was grey, o' course he weren't no chicken, anyway! And he says to me pitiful like 'Blake, I surely don't look as old as all that?'

"'You've bin ill, perfesser,' I says, 'and it don't make a man look younger. You'll be all right when you've had a bath there's plenty o' water now.'

"Well, I could see 'e weren't satisfied, because he gives a bit of a groan, and looks at hisself in the glass agin. But a day or two arterwards he was well enough to get up, and when he sees Erongo for the fust time, with the water a-pouring down that big fall, he brightens up at once.

"'Just the very place the very place. Who knows but it may be true? Never to be old! . . . Never to be old!' I hears him a-saying, over and over again; but nat'rally, I on'y thought he was a bit off his napper, same as half these 'ere perfessers is, wot think they know heverythink! Anyhow, as soon as ever he was able, oft he goes and bathes in the stream, farther up, a goodish way from the camp, and a power o' good it seemed to do him, for he comes back a-looking ten years younger. Next day he sends the two prospectors out fer a long trip and then he calls me.

"'Jim,' says he, "ow do you think I look?'

"'Look?' I says for I was fair mazed at the look of him, 'why ten years younger than ever I seed yer!'

"'Just so,' says 'e. . . . 'It's true then!'

"'Wot's true,' I says.

"'The water of life,' says he; 'I have searched for it fer years!'

"'Take some quinine,' says I, 'and back yer goes to bed,' for I'd seen fever patients that way afore.

"'You don't know heverythink, Blake,' he says he 'ad a nasty way o' using that there expression; 'it isn't fever it's joy. For if the stream below has such an effect, wot will the source be like?'

"Well, it wasn't much good taking notice of what he said, but anyhow, next day 'e'd gone!

"The boys said he'd gone upstream towards the big fall, and arter a while I follered him. As you know, that there waterfall takes a lot of reaching, but I gets there at last, and there he was a-sitting in the stream. Lord, I 'ardly knew 'im, he looked so young and vigorous, and full o' life. He wanted me to bathe, but I'd had a wash on'y a day or two before, and I wouldn't. But, my word, he seemed to keep getting younger; and as fer strength, why on our way back he jumped over rocks like a klipbok I never seen the like! Next mornin' he'd gone agin, and this time he stays away fer two days, and I gets scared. The prospectors was away, and there was on'y me and the boys and I couldn't get 'em to go far up Erongo, for they said it was full of devils. P'raps they was right them there boys knows a lot though they don't know heverythink! Third day I gets up early and goes right up the side o' the stream, till I gets to the waterfall, but no sign did I find. And I sits there a-pondering, till all of a sudden I 'ears a voice a- calling 'Jim!'

"I turns round, and there 'e was at least I s'posed it was him! He hadn't a stitch o' clothes on, and his skin shone like a babby's. Look young? Why the only thing I knew about 'im was his voice! And he came a-bounding over the rocks as if he was made of injy-rubber. And his face was all a-shinin' it made me think o' pictures o' hangels to see him.

"'Jim! Jim!' he sings out; half a-laughing and 'alf sobbing, 'it's true! it's true! look at me I'm young agin! I'm immortal!'

"'You're naked,' I says, 'and you ought to know better at your time o' life and in this 'ere 'ot sun too!'

"He laughs like a madman.

"'Ye old fool,' he says (nice it was, and on'y yesterday he'd bin a lot older than me!). 'Don't you see it's true? I've been to the top, man, and bathed in the source there, and I'm immortal!'

"'You're barmy,' I says, though I was a bit scared, for never have I seen such a difference!

"'Come with me to the top and bathe,' says he, 'and see fer yerself!'

"'Who's to take me?' I says. 'I ain't a bird!'

"'I will!' he shouts; and before you could 'a' said 'Jack Robinson,' he grabs 'old of me in a clove hitch!

"I was strong and a bit useful in them days, but I was like a babby in the arms of a giant, and he tucked me under one arm and 'eld me like a parcel. And then well! I know yer don't believe it, but yer don't know he very think. He jist went up the side of that there cliff like a klip-springer, catching on to little points of rock, and a-springing from place to place, as if I didn't weigh more'n a feather; with me under his arm a-hollering blue murder, and a-lookin' down sick and dizzy, and a-praying for him not to let me fall! Right up that there cliff as you can see from here we went, and almost afore I knew what had happened, I was on top. There was thick grass, and bush, and flowers, and tall trees and fruit I'd never seen afore, and butterflies everywhere, and he sat me down jist close to the brink, and there I sat a-gasping. And then he laughed and what a laugh it was jist like a trumpet ringing out, and he says again: 'Come and bathe, man, and be immortal, like me!'

"And then he hustles me off into the wood, flustered and frightened, and a wondering when I should get down to terra-cotta agin. That there mountain ain't flat on top, its cup-shaped, and it's only the rim you can see from here; and there's trees and water everywhere, and birds a-singing, and flowers a-blooming and butterflies a-flitting, and if there'd o'ny bin a nice little pub up there, like wot I knows of there at 'ome in Lime'ouse, it would 'a' bin Parrydise and I'd 'a' stayed. We sees no animals and no snakes, and we goes along the banks of the stream, and at last we conies to a deep pool that bubbled and fizzed up like soda water, all over.

"'The Source!' he says; 'the Source!' an' you could ha' 'eard 'is voice a mile off; 'the Water of Life! I bathed here this morning look at me! Come, bathe, old fool, and be young, and a companion fer me, and we'll stay here fer ever!'

"'Course, I knew he must be barmy though 'ow he got me up that cliff certainly is a mystery! Any'ow, I thought I'd better 'umour 'im a bit. So I starts to undress; and then I pauses.

"'Any beer here?' I asks.

"'Beer, what do you want vile beer for, when there's necktie fit fer the gords to drink?' says 'e.

"'Baccy?' I asks agin knowin' he 'ated it.

"'Phaw,' he says, 'your filthy smoke what need is there of it?'

"'Wimmen!' I says, thinkin' that would be a clincher fer him.

"'Yes,' he shouts; 'beautiful nymphs, spirits as immortal as myself!'

"'I don't see 'em!' says I.

"'They are in the water,' says he; 'beautiful water nymphs and wood nymphs lurks there among the trees! Bathe, fool, and your eyes will be opened!'

"That settled it. I'd got an argyment fer 'im now.

"'Not me,' I says, putting my shirt on agin. 'No beer; no baccy; no wimmen but a lot o' shameless huzzies a-hiding and a-waiting to watch a feller bathe! Not me. I go back besides, I 'ad a bath on'y a few days ago.'

"Well, 'e was that wild I thought 'e'd chuck me in, but I 'umored and coaxed 'im for I had to get 'im to take me down again; and at last 'e did. How he did it I don't know, for when he took me up, like a kid, I shut me eyes, and never opened 'em agin till he put me down at the foot of the waterfall.

"'Good-bye, fool,' he said; 'some day you'll be sorry!'

"Well, we never seen 'im agin, and when I told the prospectors wot I'd seen, they told me to put more water in my grog. And at last the whole outfit went back and reported the perfesser lost or dead.

"But I knows better: he's up there yet! Look! see that smoke on the top? Well, who's a-goin' to make a fire on Erongo if it ain't 'im? You don't know heverythink, if yer thinks yer does."